CW01091317

The Secret Six

The Treasure of Shadowmere Island

Contents

Acknowledgements

I want to thank everyone who helped me write this book.

My wife, who once again put up with my distracted mind while working on it and the many hours I spent at the keyboard.

Christopher John Payne, who taught me so much and to whom I owe an outstanding debt of gratitude.

My grandsons, who are my best critics and the many others who encouraged me.

About the Author

 Stephen Nuttall is a father and a grandfather who has entertained his children and grandchildren for many years with his stories. He is a former police officer and Criminal Investigator.

"I am looking for someone to share in an adventure that I am arranging, and it's very difficult to find anyone."

J.R.R. Tolkien, The Hobbit

The Secret Six are:
Freddie, Josh, Harper, Leo, Noz and Jack the dog.
Their first adventure together is told in the book

The Adventure at Smugglers' Cove

If you have enjoyed this book, you will also like

The Lighthouse of Adventure
(Due December 2023)

Chapter One

Bad News

"I've got some bad news," said Freddie Dubois with a frown. He was in the shed at the bottom of his garden, where the Secret Six met. Freddie was tall, with blonde hair that hung over his eyes, causing him to flick it out of the way occasionally. He wore a blue shirt with rolled-up sleeves, trainers, and jeans.

His twin brother, Joshua, known as Josh, sat across from him on an upturned wooden box. He wore a dark green shirt and black jeans.

Their dad was Alexandre, known as Alex. He was French, working for the Government as a special agent, while their mum was English.

Both boys spoke fluent French to the confusion of their mum when they and their dad talked together.

Harper Lyon, her brother Leo, and Noah Khumalo sat in a semi-circle around them.

Harper was tall and slim, with her hair in a ponytail. She was dressed in blue jeans and a long-sleeved red shirt.

Her brother, Leo, was the smallest and quietest of his friends. He had brown hair and was wearing dark trousers and a white T-shirt.

Noah, known as Noz, wore a blue-checked shirt and light-coloured trousers.

Their loyal cocker spaniel dog, Jack, lay beside Harper, covering his eyes with his paws. He had been a bomb and gun search dog, working with the twins' dad when he'd been a policeman. Using his fantastic sense of smell, he'd found many hidden explosives and firearms during his time as a working dog. He was also fearless; though not a big dog, he would guard the children with his life.

"I've got some bad news," Freddie said.

He sounded serious, making everyone sit up and pay attention. Even Noz stopped in mid-bite of his chocolate bar.

"Whatever's the matter?" Harper asked, concerned. Freddie seemed really upset. His voice was quite shaky as he answered. "We're moving away from here. Mum and Dad, Jack, Josh, and me."

There was complete silence as the awful news sank in.

"What? Why? Where?" Leo asked quickly.

"You can't!" Harper exclaimed. "What about the Secret Six? And what about little Jack? You can't just go off somewhere else!" Tears welled up in her eyes. Sensing the distress in the children's voices, Jack sat up and moved closer to Harper. She buried her face in his fur for comfort.

"Where are you moving to?" Noz asked.

"Cumbria," Josh replied, speaking for the first time. "It's right up in the Northwest of the country."

"But why?" Harper sniffed. "Why do you have to move?"

"It's because of our house," Freddie explained. "It's a house Dad rented when he joined the police force. We've been happy here, so he never discussed us buying our own. But he now works for the government in London and has to hand the house

10

back to the police authority."

"We thought we'd be here forever," added Josh.

"So why doesn't your dad buy a house in the village?" Noz puzzled. "Why move all that way up north?"

"It's not that easy. It's too expensive around here. And besides, we have a cousin who owns a place in Cumbria. She's gone abroad for a few years and is letting us stay there until she returns. It's also better for Dad's job."

The children sat silently, feeling miserable after hearing the news, the weekend's excitement vanishing in a moment.

Leo said, "Even though adventures are scary, I had secretly hoped we'd stumble upon another one."

"But if you leave and take little Jack with you," Noz said sadly, "there won't be a Secret Six or adventures anymore."

They had first called themselves the Secret Six during their last school holiday and their first exciting adventure in Cornwall.[1]

"We can't be the Secret Three," Harper insisted. "It just won't be the same!"

"Remember," Leo chimed in, "you said we needed all our skills. So often that we got tired of hearing it!"

Freddie was a natural leader who was skillful in **deciphering** coded messages and had a blue belt in Judo.

Josh was interested in maps and liked to study them, especially the ancient ones. He was also quite knowledgeable about the night sky.

[1] The Adventure at Smugglers' Cove

11

He knew the names of most of the stars and could tell where the north lay just by looking up at them, and would often wander about the fields after dark. His dad had trained him to move through the woods without being seen or heard.

He frequently used French words and phrases in his conversation, and Freddie constantly reminded him that most people had no idea what he was talking about.

But he continued doing it, anyway.

Harper was the fastest runner by far out of all of them, except for Jack the dog, and was a brave and talented climber and athlete.

Leo had a fantastic ability as a **ventriloquist** and imitator of people's voices. He could 'throw' his voice so that it seemed to come from behind a door or inside a cupboard, and he could **mimic** voices so well that they were indistinguishable from that of the actual people.

Noz had a hobby of doing tricks and could pick your pocket or even remove your wristwatch without you feeling a thing. Freddie would tease him and call him their 'criminal,' something that he was secretly pleased about.

He had a habit of frequently polishing his glasses. He would whip them off and buff them up on his hanky. Sometimes, they even seemed to have a mind of their own, and they would slide down his nose. But he had a trick up his sleeve—his finger! He'd nudge them back into their rightful place with a quick flick. When he was excited, he would wave them about to make his point.

He also had a **voracious** appetite and was constantly

12

hungry and looking for food.

Freddie let out a sigh. "We're sorry. We don't want to leave. You've become such amazing friends, and I don't think we'll ever find others like you."

Josh looked at his twin brother and smiled. "But there is some *bonnes nouvelles*—good news. We're not moving until after the school break. And our parents have said you can come with us to the new house for the holiday if you want to."

"Although Dad will be away at work," Freddie added, not bothering to pull his twin up on his use of French for once, "so it'll be just Mum taking care of us. I'm not sure how she will handle all of us, though!"

"And just to add to that," said Josh, "there is no Wi-Fi at the house, and it's in a poor reception area. Dad's cousin is a bit of a **recluse** and lives in the past. She has only recently had central heating put in. Apparently, she doesn't like the modern world, so there isn't even a landline. So there's no point in bringing any devices or mobile phones."

"I think some time without social media will be good," said Harper. "If we want to do something different and have an adventure, perhaps those things will get in the way?"

"Adventures will only come to us when we get out and about and use our eyes and minds to think along different lines," said Noz, polishing his glasses furiously. "I don't mind living in the past for a while, if it means we will all be together."

So that was agreed, and instantly, the mood among the children changed. The sad reality of the Dubois family moving was in the future. For now, they had the present moment and the chance to spend the entire holiday together!

"If we want?" Harper beamed. "If?"

She jumped to her feet and embraced Freddie and Josh happily. "Of course, we want to come! That would be absolutely amazing, and I can't think of anything else I'd rather do!"

And, of course, the others agreed enthusiastically, including Jack, who wagged his tail energetically.

Chapter Two

Swiftwater Jack

The twins' mum had hired a big van to move boxes of personal belongings to their future home in Cumbria, so there was room for the five children and Jack to travel with her.

Freddie and Josh bagged the front seats beside their mum, and the others squeezed into the back with Jack. The journey was long and hot, but finally, they arrived at their destination. But not without a minor mishap as they turned into the lane leading to their new home.

A rough-looking, open-backed lorry came speeding out of the junction, almost colliding with them. Two men were sitting in the front, although only the driver was visible. He was a thin, weasel-faced man wearing a scruffy baseball cap. He swerved onto the grass **verge** to avoid a collision and shouted at Mrs Dubois angrily. Shaking his fist, he accelerated fast along the road in a cloud of **acrid** black smoke before disappearing into the distance.

"Well, I never," breathed the twins' mum, as calm as a cucumber. "That must be the most awful driving I've seen in a long time!"

"*Quel idiot*—what an idiot!" exclaimed Josh.

But it was all quickly forgotten as they halted at the end of a stony driveway, and Harper cried out, "There it is!"

15

Everyone scrambled out of the van, relieved to stretch their legs after the long drive. Before them stood a magnificent white cottage with a roof so low that it almost hid the ground-floor windows with its thatch. It was like something out of a fairy tale.

Beyond the cottage, at the bottom of the cliffs, lay a strip of sandy gravel, followed by a vast ribbon of blue water that extended to the distant shore, shrouded in mist. It was dotted with several islands of various sizes. Some were just rocky outcrops, while others were green, boasting forests of trees and wide grassy fields.

One island in particular, far in the distance, captured Freddie's attention. It stood out, surrounded by steep, rugged rocks, as if defending itself against invaders.

"It looks wild!" Leo chimed in.

Without wasting another moment, Noz shouted, "Let's explore!" And just like that, the children scattered, their laughter echoing through the air.

"Wait a moment. Weren't you going to help me unload the boxes?"

Smiling, the twins' mum understood how happy they were, especially after having to go their separate ways after the holidays. She followed the children into the coolness of the old cottage, carefully avoiding the heavy timber beams crossing the ceiling.

"Let's have tea," she declared, "and afterwards, you can assist me in unloading the van. There will be time for exploration later."

"The six of us are looking forward to doing that!" said Josh.

"Six? There are only five of you," replied his mother.

"You're forgetting our little Jack," Josh said. "He's one of us and takes part in our adventures."

"Oh no," his mother replied, shaking her head. "You won't find any of those risky adventure things here. This isn't like Cornwall. This will be a peaceful holiday!"

Seated in the dining room, the children marvelled at the feast she had so quickly prepared. Bottles of cola, ham and cheese sandwiches, crisps, chocolate bars, and a bowl of fruit awaited them.

In the kitchen, a large bowl of chunky meat and dog biscuits was set aside for Jack, who seemed slightly put out at having to eat in a separate room. Nevertheless, everyone enjoyed their meal, and afterwards, all the boxes were carried inside and piled up in the living room.

"Now, let's explore!" decided Freddie, and the Six dashed upstairs.

The roof on the upper floor was also low, and they had to be careful not to bump into the beams across the ceiling.

"People must have been shorter when this place was built," Harper observed. "I've already hit my head twice!"

Leo chimed in, "Wow! Look how this floor slopes. The end of the bed has been propped up on wooden blocks to make it level!"

"You'd roll out of it otherwise," commented Noz. They had explored the entire top floor in no time, each child claiming their bedroom. Noz and Leo decided on the room overlooking the back garden, while Freddie and Josh opted for the one with a view of the lake.

Harper found herself in the smallest bedroom at the end of the corridor. However, she didn't mind, since Mrs Dubois had thoughtfully placed Jack's basket beside her bed for company, and both Jack and Harper were delighted with that arrangement.

Suddenly, Josh called out, "Come and see this! In the front bedroom!"

Everyone rushed in, with Jack wagging his tail excitedly, wondering what all the fuss was about.

"Look at the painting on the wall!"

He pointed to a dark oil painting of a weather-beaten sailor from a far-off era, with collar-length hair, a rugged black beard, and a three-cornered hat atop his head. The sailor wore a light-coloured, long-sleeved shirt covered by a black coat. He held a clay pipe in one hand while the other was tucked into his pocket as he stood gazing at something in the far distance. Underneath the picture, his name was written. Swiftwater Jack.

"He looks like a pirate," Harper declared, her eyes wide with fascination.

"Or a smuggler. And to think he used to live here!" said Josh.

"How do *you* know?" questioned Leo.

"*C'est simple*—it's simple. The name over the front door," chided Josh. "You're not very observant for a member of the Secret Six!"

"I'll check," responded Harper, as she dashed down the stairs to the front door.

Freddie opened the window and leaned out. "Well?"

"Swiftwater," she shouted up. "The name of the cottage is Swiftwater!"

SWIFTWATER JACK

Chapter Three

The Island

"Let's explore outside," Leo suggested once they had thoroughly inspected every nook and cranny of the cottage.

"Wait! I need my binoculars," Freddie exclaimed. He hurried into his bedroom and emerged with them hanging around his neck. "Okay, all set. Let's go!" With Jack leading the way, they ventured into the front garden. And as they stepped outside, an incredible view unfolded before their eyes. The mist had cleared, revealing a breathtaking sight of the lake, the distant shore, and the enchanting islands.

"Wow, that's epic!" Noz exclaimed, his eyes widening with awe. "What a place to live!"

"Don't remind us," Freddie sighed. "The view might be awesome, but we won't be together, will we?"

"I'm sorry, guys," responded Noz. "I forgot about that in all the excitement."

"We just have to make the most of the time we have," Harper reassured them, her voice filled with determination, "and it's okay to enjoy being here."

Leo pointed towards one of the islands. "Look! There's something on that island. A building or something."

They followed his gaze, and Freddie looked through the binoculars.

"Spectacular!" he said. "It's a ruin: a castle or a

21

church. Can we get to it?" he asked.

"Absolutely not," said Leo. "For a start, we don't have a boat."

"Perhaps we could borrow one?" suggested Harper. "Does anyone have any experience with boats?"

"Freddie and I have done quite a bit of sailing with our dad in the past," said Josh. "Just small dinghies, nothing big. We used to go every summer until he got too busy with work. But I'm confident that we can soon pick it up again."

"I've had a little experience, too," informed Noz. "Our family used to go on holiday to the Norfolk Broads and hire a boat."

"This isn't exactly a river," stated Leo firmly. "It could be dangerous out there on the water."

"I wonder if there's anything in the house that will tell us about the island," pondered Freddie as the children trooped back inside.

"*Maman*—Mum," cried Josh, "where are you?"

She hurried down the stairs, a pile of sheets and towels in her arms.

"I'm here; what's up?" she said breathlessly.

"Nothing," replied Freddie. "We were just wondering whether there is anything in the cottage that can tell us about the area. You know, maps, tourist leaflets, books. Stuff like that."

"Goodness," said his mother, "you gave me quite a turn. From all that shouting, I thought something was wrong!"

"What could possibly be wrong?" answered Leo. "You said yourself that this is a quiet place!"

She looked suspiciously at him. "Just watch out. I will be keeping a careful eye on all of you!"

Then she smiled good-humouredly. "But yes, there are some brochures and maps in the **bureau** over there."

She pointed to the corner of the sitting room. "Just make sure you don't get involved in any madcap adventures. I'm not sure if I can manage that at the moment."

"No, Mum," said Freddie and Josh together.

She went back upstairs, unconvinced about the twins' assurances. She knew their passion for adventure had worsened since the Secret Six was formed. [1] It was just as well she had never found out the whole story.

"You take the brochures," suggested Freddie to Harper, "and you take the maps, Josh. You're the best with them."

"Leo, why don't you look through the bookcase and see what you can find? Noz, you and I can scout through the cottage again and see if we can find any papers or old books that may help."

There was silence for a couple of hours while the children went about their tasks.

Freddie and Noz wandered around the cottage, first downstairs and then upstairs, poking in cupboards and drawers and looking for anything that might give them a clue as to the significance of the island and the cottage named after a man who looked like a pirate.

"There's nothing here," announced Noz. "We'd better go downstairs and see what the others have found."

"Slow down," ordered Mrs Dubois, who happened to

[1] The Adventure at Smugglers' Cove

be coming up the stairs, this time carrying a large cardboard box. "What's the great hurry? Be careful; otherwise, there's going to be an accident!"

The boys controlled themselves with difficulty and **sauntered** down the remaining few stairs. But the minute she disappeared from view, they raced across the dining room and into the sitting room where the other members of the Secret Six had gathered.

Harper pointed to a map laid out on the floor. "We've found out something. Look! Here's the lake at the front of the cottage, and there's that big island. And there's a name."

The boys examined the map intently.

"It says Shadowmere Island," replied Freddie.

"That has jogged my memory," advised Noz. "This water is not really a lake. The proper name is a '*Mere*.' I learned that at school," he said triumphantly.

"So, Shadowmere means a shadow on the water?" said Leo.

"Possibly, but that's not all we found," continued Harper.

She handed Josh a folded sheet of paper. "I don't quite know what it is. It's a bit like a map, but has lots of lines and marks on it."

He examined it, and his eyes lit up excitedly as he recognised it. "It's a chart," he exclaimed, "showing what appears to be a safe passage across the lake— sorry, *Mere*—to the island!"

Chapter Four

A Confession

In a flash, the day had flown by, and darkness was falling.

"Bedtime," instructed the twins' mum, and the children were too tired to argue.

Jack was up the stairs in an instant, and by the time the children had all brushed their teeth and changed into their nightclothes, he was curled up in his basket next to Harper's bed, fast asleep.

Freddie had trouble sleeping, however. The painting of Swiftwater Jack and the irresistible presence of the mysterious-looking island across the water was playing on his mind.

He shifted restlessly in his bed and eventually got up in frustration. Creeping over to the window, he drew back the curtains quietly to avoid disturbing his twin and looked out.

It was a clear night, and the stars could be seen so clearly, hanging low in the sky. But what was that in the distance? Not a star, surely? It seemed a bit too low for that.

He took a moment before he realised it was moving. Someone was on the island!

"Josh!" He ran over to his brother and shook him. "Josh, wake up!"

His twin stirred and groaned, sitting up and rubbing his eyes.

"Whatever is it? I was having the most spectacular dream."

"There's someone on Shadowmere," said Freddie urgently. "I just saw a light. Quick, come and look!"

Josh was out of bed instantly and peered intently out the window.

"Where?" he asked doubtfully. "I can't see anything. Only stars."

"It was there a moment ago; I saw it!" assured Freddie. "Here, let me see."

He opened the window and looked out into the night. But there was now nothing to be seen.

"If it was a bright orange-coloured star, very low and scraping the treetops, it was probably the planet Mars," asserted Josh. He got back into bed, pulled the covers over his head, and was fast asleep again in no time.

Freddie was speechless. And he was annoyed. He knew that what he'd seen wasn't a silly old planet. And it definitely hadn't been orange. He made up his mind there and then. The Secret Six just had to get to Shadowmere Island somehow. Something was going on out there. It really was most unusual for someone to be poking about on an uninhabited island at night. Despite his mother's assurance of a quiet holiday, it seemed it might not be!

The following morning, Freddie could hardly wait to tell the others about what he'd witnessed during the night.

Sitting at the breakfast table, Josh was still insistent. "I saw nothing," he assured the others. "As I told Freddie, it was most likely Mars, which is very low in the sky. It's easy to mistake it for a light."

"Does Mars move?" queried Harper.

"Not really. You wouldn't notice it," replied Josh. Harper turned to Freddie. "Are you sure it was moving?" she questioned. "Is it possible that it was just a star? We all want an adventure, but let's not be too hasty and imagine things that aren't there!"

"Hasty?" spluttered Freddie. "Imagine? I know what I saw, and the light *was* moving. It was more than just a light. It was more like a *beam* of light."

"Like a powerful torch?" suggested Harper.

"That's exactly it!" exclaimed Freddie. "It must have been a torch."

"We can't get out to the island anyway," cautioned Leo, "so it's not worth discussing."

"That's not like you, Leo," pointed out Noz. "I thought you were keen on an adventure?"

Leo remained silent.

"There's one way to settle this," reasoned Harper, "and that's for us to go out there and check it out. What do you think? Those in favour, put your hands up."

Four hands immediately went up.

"Leo?" said Harper. "You don't want to investigate Swiftwater Jack's Island?"

Leo was silent for a moment, looking embarrassed. "Okay, I'll be honest with you all. I'm too nervous."

"You nervous?" responded Josh in unbelief. "I've never known you to be frightened of an adventure!"

Leo took a deep breath before replying. "It's because I can't swim!" he confessed.

Harper was the first to break the silence. "I didn't know that," she declared. "You seemed okay in the water when we went on holiday with Mum and Dad."

"I just splashed around in the shallows with my foot on the bottom," he admitted.

"There's a simple solution to that," declared Freddie. "We'll teach you!"

"I'm not so sure," replied Leo. "Teachers at school have tried, but I've been too scared to trust them."

"Leave it to us," declared Noz, "we'll have you swimming like a fish in no time!"

"First thing tomorrow," promised Josh. "So, let's go down to the beach and sus it out, shall we?"

Steep wooden steps led from the clifftop down to the broad strip of sand below. Jack was hesitant, so Freddie picked him up in his arms and carried him down.

He was rewarded with a lick on the cheek as he set him down on the beach.

"You be the new people moving into the captain's cottage?" A man's voice cut across the sound of the waves tumbling onto the beach.

Sitting on a canvas stool by the water's edge and partly hidden by a large rock was a grizzled, elderly man holding a fishing rod. He scratched his head underneath his woollen hat as Josh and Freddie went over to him.

Jack got there first and wagged his tail to greet the stranger.

"I'm Josh, and this is my brother Freddie. We'll be moving in with our mum and dad after the school holidays. These are our friends."

The old man nodded, his bright eyes staring at them, unflinching.

"Nice dog," he said, ruffling Jack's long ears without

taking his eyes off the children.

"We were wondering about the island across the far side of the *Mere*," said Noz. "Is it private, or are visitors allowed?"

"So, you're interested in the island?" said the man, turning the reel on his rod as he wound in the line before laying it down on the pebbles.

He stood up, and for the first time, the children saw he was wearing black waders that came right to the top of his thighs.

He walked awkwardly up to them. "If you want my advice," he announced, "I'd keep away from there. Folk around here say that Swiftwater Jack sails his ghost ship to the island in the dead of night!"

Freddie laughed. "We don't believe in ghosts," he declared.

The old man shook his head. "Many's the time he's been seen," he insisted.

"We'd still like to visit. How can we get there?" insisted Harper. "Is there a local that will take us?"

"You won't find many around here that will go there for love or money," the old man cautioned, "especially after dark!" With that, he returned to his stool and fishing rod.

"But the light..." began Leo, thinking of what Freddie said he'd seen on the island during the night. Freddie stopped him with a warning glance. "No matter, but thank you," he said politely to the old man. "We'll find a way."

The fisherman gave a loud sigh at the determination of the children.

"Don't say I didn't warn you," he informed them,

"but if you really must go, take that boat there." He pointed to a wooden dinghy pulled up onto the beach in the shadow of the cliff.

"We can't take someone's boat," replied Noz. "That would be stealing."

"The boat belongs to you if you own the cottage, for all the good it will do you," the old man snorted. "And if you are foolhardy enough to try to get to the island, on your heads be it!"

"But," repeated Harper, "is it private? We don't want to get into trouble with the owner by trespassing."

"It's private," he answered, "but no one knows who it belongs to now. The last owner was Captain Jack."

"So," said Freddie, by way of **clarity**, "if nobody owns it, we can explore it, and no one can stop us?"

The old man gave them a curious look. "No one ever traced Captain Jack's last will after he died—and many have tried. Shadowmere Island has been waiting for its rightful owner to be discovered all these years."

"We could find it!" shouted Leo in excitement. "We could discover the lost will of Jack Swiftwater after all these centuries."

"You'll have to be quick then," said the fisherman. "A businessman from out of town has offered to buy it from the authorities, and they have agreed because there is no chance of anyone coming forward to claim it after all this time."

And with that, he picked up his stool and fishing rod and walked clumsily in his waders along the beach and out of sight.

"We'd best explore Shadowmere before it's sold then," said Josh. "The new owner probably wouldn't allow it."

"So we'd best not talk about our plans or mention lights on islands, Leo!" warned Freddie.

The Secret Six crowded around the small boat. "This is yours, twins!" exclaimed Harper.

"I don't think so," replied Freddie. "It belongs to the house, and we're just looking after it while Dad's cousin is abroad."

"It's ours for now, anyway," exclaimed Josh. "Look, it's got a name painted on it."

He pulled the tarp cover back to reveal the stern.

"It's called '*Swiftwater*!" he breathed.

Chapter Five

The Weasel

Once they'd returned to the cottage, the children gathered to figure out their next steps. Noz, as always, full of ideas, spoke up first.

"Maybe we should learn more about our pirate captain," he suggested, eager to unravel the mystery. Freddie nodded in agreement. "And we should also learn more about the island," he added.

Still bewildered by the warning about ghosts from the fisherman on the beach, Harper couldn't believe what she had heard. "Ghosts? That's just crazy!" she exclaimed.

Josh chimed in gently, "Well, the people who live here believe in them."

"Perhaps that's the explanation for the lights you saw, Freddie," said Harper.

Josh was a bit taken aback. "Not Mars then, but ghosts?" he responded incredulously.

"Not ghosts," responded Harper. "But perhaps superstitious people saw the lights and thought they were ghosts!"

Freddie turned to Leo, who had been unusually quiet. "Leo, any ideas?" he asked, concerned.

Leo sighed and replied, "I'm sorry." With that, he hurried upstairs to his room.

"It's this swimming thing," responded Harper. "I know my brother, and he feels he's letting everyone

35

down."

"Well, he's not," replied Josh firmly. "We'll get him swimming in no time, and then you'll see. He'll soon be the old Leo again!"

"I hope so," said Harper. "I haven't seen him quite so upset before."

"I'm going up to talk to him," decided Freddie, and so saying, he went upstairs.

He was gone a long time, and when he came down, Leo was following behind.

"It's okay now," said Leo.

"What did you say?" asked Noz, taking his glasses off and giving them a quick clean on the corner of his shirt.

"That doesn't matter," replied Freddie, looking apologetic. "Sorry to sound secretive, but it was a private talk between Leo and me. I hope you all understand."

And that was that.

With everything settled, Harper took charge of the situation. "Let's search the cottage again," she suggested. "Leo and Josh, perhaps you could look through the brochures and papers again for any details about the island? And Freddie, would you and Noz do the same for information about Captain Jack?"

The boys split up to begin their searches while Harper headed outside with Jack, the dog.

"Come on, boy," she called. "Let's see if we can find any clues together."

Leo and Josh began their search through the pile of books and leaflets stuffed inside the bureau.

"Your cousin has collected loads of stuff," observed

Leo.

"*C'est vrai*—it's true," replied Josh. "But that might be just what we need. There's more chance of us finding out about Shadowmere Island."

"Your cousin—who is she, anyway?" asked Leo.

"I've no idea," replied Josh. "She's Dad's cousin, really. I know she's a historian or something, but that's about all I know."

"A historian?" responded Leo. "That might mean lots of old documents somewhere in the house."

"Could be," said Josh. "Keep searching."

The boys gradually worked their way through the pile in front of them. They were halfway through, but there was no mention of Shadowmere Island.

"We should have questioned that old fisherman more," declared Leo. "I bet he knows things!"

"I'm not sure he'd tell us, though," responded Josh. "He was more concerned about us running into Captain Swiftwater's ghost!"

They laughed as they continued their search.

"Here's an old book that looks interesting," said Leo, passing the leather-bound volume to Josh. "It's about the people that lived along the shore of the *Mere* a few hundred years ago."

"Does it mention Shadowmere?" questioned Josh.

"I can't see anything," responded Leo.

"Ok, put it in the 'to check' pile for later," answered Josh, and the boys continued their **browsing**.

They were interrupted by Freddie and Noz bursting into the room.

"Where's Harper?" queried Freddie.

"She went outside to see if there were any clues. I

haven't heard her come back. But she's got Jack with her, so she'll be fine," said Leo.

"What have you found?" asked Josh.

"Let's go and find Harper first," suggested Freddie, "and then we can share this."

The four boys made their way outside into the garden.

"Harper!" called out Leo. "Where have you got to?" There was no response.

"Harper," shouted Leo again, "can you hear us?"

"I know what to do," said Freddie, and he went back into the house.

He hurried upstairs and rummaged through his suitcase until he found what he was looking for. He was halfway down the stairs when he saw the man in the hallway crouched over the pile of papers.

It was the weasel-faced man in the cap who had almost run them off the road in his truck the day before.

His name was Jamie Jenkins, known, especially to the police, as Jamie 'The Weasel' Jenkins because of his thin, pinched-looking face.

"Hey!" shouted Freddie, leaping down the remaining stairs.

The man stood up quickly, and Freddie saw he was holding the leather-bound book that Leo had found.

"Give that to me!" yelled Freddie, but the man ran for the front door, clutching it tightly.

His shouting had alerted the others, and they came rushing through the door just as the thief tried to exit. Seeing the way blocked, he turned and ran back towards Freddie, an aggressive look on his face.

All he saw was a young boy in front of him, and he

charged at Freddie, expecting to knock him flying so that he could escape through the back of the house.

But with his judo training, Freddie instinctively stepped to one side, thrusting out his right arm and grabbing the intruder's coat.

The moment that his hand made contact, something entirely unexpected happened. In a swift move, he bent his knees and stepped in, at the same time with his left hand seizing the man's wrist. Without effort, he turned on the ball of his foot, spinning the surprised man straight off his feet and over his shoulder. He flew into the air until, with a cry of pain, he landed solidly on his back on the hard stone floor.

"I'll take that," said Freddie firmly, removing the book from the stunned thief's hand.

"What's going on?" cried Josh as the others gathered around the fallen man.

"I caught him going through our papers," answered Freddie, "and he had this book."

"That's from our 'to check' pile said Josh crossly.

Then, without warning, the would-be thief leapt to his feet, pushed roughly past Noz, and disappeared out of the front door.

"Let him go," said Noz, "he won't bother us again."

"He'll be driving that truck like an idiot again," promised Freddie, "just like the other day."

Noz laughed. "No, he won't be doing that," he assured them.

Freddie stared him in the eye. "Don't tell me, you haven't…?"

"Oh yes, I have," said Noz. "The brute of a man almost knocked me to the floor, so I took his keys to teach him a lesson!"

"You picked his pocket?" spluttered Josh.

Noz jangled a bunch of keys in front of them. "I think I may have done just that," he said. "He won't be driving his truck anywhere just yet!"

"I think he's probably learnt his lesson several times over," suggested Josh. "Did you see that judo throw?"

"It was nothing," asserted Freddie modestly. "Forget about that."

"Just as well you went back to the cottage," said Noz. "What made you do that?"

Freddie reached into his pocket. "It's Jack's dog whistle," he informed them. "When we were looking for Harper, I thought if I got Jack to come back, she would follow. But the important thing is, why was that man poking around here, and why did he try to steal this book?"

He held it up as Jack bounded through the door, closely followed by Harper.

"What's going on?" she asked. "Have I missed anything?"

Chapter Six

Leo Takes the Plunge

The boys brought Harper up to date with what had happened.

"What cheek," she fumed, "how dare he!"

"Should we tell Mum?" asked Josh.

"You know how she feels about adventures," responded Freddie. "I think it is best if we keep this to ourselves. But we must certainly be more careful in the future."

"But it means that something is up," maintained Harper. "Otherwise, why would that awful man sneak into our cottage?"

"What about that chart we found," said Josh. "Did we put it somewhere safe? With someone determined to take our maps and papers, we'd better take better care of them."

Harper rummaged through the documents on the table. "It's here," she said.

"Phew!" said Leo, "Just as well he didn't find it."

Freddie took it and handed it to Harper. "You keep it safe," he said. "No one will take it now."

"He desperately wanted this book," said Josh, holding it up. "So, there must be something in here that's important to someone."

He unwrapped the leather thong from around it, opened it, and laid it on the dining room table. The pages inside were yellow and fragile with age; the

41

ink faded and barely readable.

"I can't make anything out," complained Noz, removing his glasses and polishing them vigorously. "The words are almost impossible to read."

"Wait! I remember seeing—" Leo didn't finish his sentence but ran upstairs to Freddie and Josh's bedroom.

He returned seconds later, holding a magnifying glass.

"I thought I'd seen one of these somewhere," he said. "It might help."

"*Parfait*—perfect!" said Josh. "Go on, Leo; it was your idea, so tell us what the book says."

Leo held the magnifying glass over the page. "It's in peculiar old English, but it mentions the cottage and the fact that the owner disappeared one night, and no one ever discovered what happened to him."

"Any names?" asked Harper.

He turned the pages and peered once more through the glass.

"Looks like it was owned by a trader, a merchant named William Cooper," he read. "This is wild," Leo continued. "Listen to this. It seems to be a record from some court in 1680. I can't quite make out the words. It looks like Kings Bench. Would that be right?" He examined the page again.

"I remember hearing about courts in history at school," confirmed Noz, "and I'm sure that the Court of Kings Bench was one of the early ones in the 17th century."

Freddie shrugged. "Never heard of it," he confessed, "but if Noz thinks it's a court, then a court it is!"

"Come on," pleaded Josh impatiently, "just tell us

what it says. I don't care whether it was a king's bench or a king's chair. What does it say?"

Noz laughed. "Not that sort of bench. It means the actual court where a judge **presided**!"

Leo continued looking at the yellowing page. "I can't read it word for word," he said. "It's too difficult. But I can make out roughly what it means."

"Please," said Harper, "get on with it!"

"This account is from a statement made by a witness after William Cooper went missing. The locals believed he was a fabulously rich miser who never spent a penny and **hoarded** all the money he made. Several people claimed they were his heirs and that the cottage and any money should go to them."

Leo went silent and read ahead for a few pages while the others waited impatiently.

"Mr Cooper had a boat that he used for trading, and he came and went along the water mostly at night."

"He sounds a bit more like a smuggler than a businessman," said Freddie.

"Anyway," continued Leo, "the cottage and everything in it went to one of the claimants. I can't see the name; the ink has faded quite a lot."

"Let me see," said Josh. "I might be able to make it out."

He took the book to the window and held the page to the light while studying it under the magnifying glass.

"Wow!" he exclaimed. "I can just see it. It looks like the successful claimant was none other than our Captain Jack Swiftwater!"

"So," said Freddie, "we have a miserly but rich

merchant who traded up and down the waterways. He went missing one day and was never seen again. Seeing as that was in the 1680s, I don't suppose he ever will be now!"

"And Jack Swiftwater took everything he had!" exclaimed Harper.

"Anything else in the book that might be useful?" queried Josh.

"Have a look, Noz," replied Leo.

Being a trickster, Noz was used to secrets—hidden compartments, secret doors, cunningly concealed hiding places in newspapers and books.

So when the book was handed to him, the first thing he did was to examine the exterior carefully, checking the binding, the spine and the cover.

He suddenly became very excited.

"Hang on, what's—"

He stopped in mid-sentence as Mrs Dubois abruptly swept into the dining room.

"Goodness, you lot," she said, "you've been loitering indoors for far too long. It's time you went out for some fresh air."

She looked at the pile of papers and books scattered across the carpet. "Whatever are you doing? she enquired.

"Checking the history of this place, Mum," said Freddie. "We're interested in who used to own it."

She looked at her son suspiciously. He wasn't usually interested in such things. But the children looked at her so innocently that she just shrugged.

"Leave all these papers and books here," she said, "and go out for an hour for some fresh air. Then back for lunch."

"Can we go swimming?" asked Josh.

Mrs Dubois knew her boys were strong swimmers, so she said, "As long as you're all careful, but check that it's safe first, and don't go too far out."

The children dashed upstairs, hurriedly changing into their swimwear and snatching their towels. The *Mere* was beckoning them with its sparkling waters, and they couldn't wait to dive in.

Jack was already ahead and met them at the top of the steps to the beach, wagging his tail eagerly.

Freddie carried him down, and Leo followed behind, his steps less enthusiastic. Anxious thoughts filled his mind as he wondered what awaited him during his swimming lessons.

"Come on, Leo!" Freddie encouraged with a grin. "It's not as scary as it seems. Who do you want to teach you?"

Leo hesitated for a moment before replying, "Maybe my sister. She's an excellent swimmer, and I trust her."

Freddie emphasised the importance of safety. "Before we jump into unknown waters," he explained, "we must check for any dangers. We must use our eyes to look out for anything that can hurt us."

He waded into the warm water and scanned the surroundings. "I don't see anything obvious," he declared. "But be careful of hidden rocks or obstacles below the surface."

He motioned for Leo to join him in the water. "We can't see everything from here," Freddie cautioned, "so we need to stay alert while swimming in places we don't know."

Leo mustered up his courage and entered the water, the waves rising to his waist. "This part is easy," he admitted, relief evident in his voice, "but putting my face underwater and taking my feet off the bottom is the scary bit!"

"Don't worry," Freddie reassured him, his voice full of confidence. "You'll get the hang of it soon enough."

Harper effortlessly swam the short distance to where they were standing. "We also have to be aware of underwater currents," she warned. "They can be strong and sweep swimmers away."

"It sounds risky before we even begin," Leo admitted with uncertainty.

"Give me your hands," Harper instructed, her voice encouraging.

Reluctantly, Leo reached out and placed his hands in Harper's grasp.

Freddie asked, "How did your school try to teach you?"

Leo groaned loudly, recalling his past swimming experiences. "It was very much jump in the deep end and make your way to the side," he replied. "That was awful. I just sunk and drank half the swimming pool!"

"That's a silly way to teach swimming," argued Harper. "No wonder you're nervous. But don't worry. With me as your teacher, you'll be swimming in no time."

Leo looked less than convinced.

Harper reassured him. "Remember, you won't sink like a stone when you take your feet off the bottom.

You'll float if you relax and don't panic."

She told Leo to stretch his legs out behind him while she continued to hold his hands. To his surprise, he discovered he floated effortlessly. A sense of achievement came over him, and a grin spread across his face.

For the next half-hour, Harper taught Leo how to move his legs and use his hands to scoop the water and propel himself forward. "Look at Jack," she pointed out. "He's doing the doggie paddle, using his paws to move forward."

"I'll leave you with Harper and Jack," declared Freddie, "while I check on the boat. You'll learn better without me around."

The sounds of laughter and splashing filled Freddie's ears as he headed toward the beached boat. He pulled back the tarp and examined it. *Swiftwater* looked sturdy and well-maintained in good condition.

The mainsail was **reefed** around the boom, and the **jib** was neatly folded inside the boat. **Stowed** on one side of the main **thwart** was a pair of oars and a lifejacket.

He re-covered the boat with the protective tarp before staring at Shadowmere Island. It was definitely mysterious and inviting. He couldn't wait to journey across the water to investigate, and their little boat seemed ready to go.

It was up to Leo now with his swimming lessons. Until he was confident, they were marooned on dry land, even though this unknown person buying the island could spoil everything. But they had all agreed after their first meeting of the Secret Six that it was either all or none of them when they went on an adventure. And this looked like it would be their last adventure anyway, so they needed to make the most of it.

Josh regularly reminded them: "We aren't the Secret four of five. We're the Secret Six."

But with the Dubois family having to live in the cottage after the holidays, soon, all that would be left would be the Secret Three.

Freddie felt a lump rise in his throat, and to overcome his sadness, he checked his watch and called out, "Time for lunch, everyone!"

The group, including Jack, climbed the steps back to the cottage, their stomachs grumbling after all the exercise.

Although cautious going down the steps, the little dog was more than capable of climbing them, and as usual, he raced ahead of everyone.

Josh couldn't contain his curiosity. "How did your swimming lessons go, Leo?"

"Okay, I guess," Leo replied, trying to sound nonchalant, but his eyes shone with a sense of achievement.

Chapter Seven

The Map

After lunch, the children washed and dried the plates before enthusiastically turning their attention once more to the mysterious book.

Mrs Dubois popped her head around the door. "I've got some things to deal with in town," she informed them, "so I'm taking the van. I'll be gone for a few hours, so you'll be on your own. Try not to get into trouble."

They waited until they heard the van start up and drive away down the track.

"You were about to say something about the book, Noz," said Freddie excitedly, "before my mum sent us all outside?"

Noz opened it and gently inserted his finger into the spine. "I thought this was a bit bulky," he said with satisfaction. "Look, there's a folded sheet of paper inside."

He carefully pulled it out and laid it on the table as the children stared at it.

"Well," said Leo at last, "isn't someone going to open it?"

"You found it, Noz," replied Josh, "so it should be you."

"It's a bit fragile," responded Noz, "and it looks like parchment. I'm afraid of it falling to bits."

"Open it slowly and carefully," advised Harper.

Noz slid it across the table to her.

"You do it, Harper," he suggested. "You're probably more nimble-fingered than me. I feel all fingers and thumbs at the moment."

Harper slowly opened the folded paper, so it lay flat on the table. She drew in her breath as a corner crumbled into dust.

"Shall I continue?" she asked hesitantly.

The others looked at each other.

"I say you continue," responded Freddie. "We have to know what's on it. It must be important, or the weasel man wouldn't have stolen it."

"Tried to steal it," corrected Josh. "He didn't get away with it, did he?"

"Whatever," said Noz. "Let's just do it."

"Everyone agreed?" asked Harper.

They all were, so she returned to the slow and meticulous opening of the ancient parchment until it was spread out on the table. She stood a cup on each corner to keep it flat.

"It's a map!" she said.

"A map of what?" asked Noz.

Everyone crowded around, and Harper had to ask them to move back.

"I can't see a thing otherwise," she protested. "It's a map of an island."

"Do you think it's Shadowmere Island?" asked Leo.

"It doesn't say," replied Harper, "and we can't tell just by looking at it."

"Who's the best at drawing?" said Freddie.

"Whatever for?" asked Josh.

"There are a lot of symbols and marks on the map," responded Freddie, "and some tiny letters that I can't make out. If, as I suspect, it all crumbles into dust if we try to fold it, we'll lose all the information. But if we can draw it accurately, it doesn't matter."

"I think that will be me," offered Harper. "I need some paper and a pencil."

Noz closed the book and moved it out of Harper's way so she could make a copy of the chart.

They sat there for a while, watching Harper sketch. Josh bent forward, leaning his arm on the book as he did so, and Freddie watched him, his face screwed up in concentration.

"That's it!" he shouted suddenly. "I just knew I'd seen it before. Come on, all of you upstairs."

He ran out of the dining room and up the stairs, mounting them two at a time, followed by Jack, who had got caught up in the excitement. The others sat bewildered for a moment before following him up to his bedroom.

"It's this painting of Swiftwater Jack," announced Freddie. "When I first saw it, I thought it was important. I just couldn't work out what it was."

"He looks a bit fierce," said Harper.

"He seems to be staring at something," mused Freddie as he stood before the painting. Turning his back, he assumed the same pose as Captain Jack, his right arm resting on the low bookcase against the wall, his left hand in his pocket.

When he set his face at the same angle as the pirate, he found he was looking out of the bedroom window across the water.

"I think the picture was painted here, in this very room," said Freddie excitedly. "Look, he was gazing

51

out across the water!"

He went over and looked out. He could see in the distance the island framed in the window.

"No, that's not it. He wasn't looking at the water," he said. "He was staring at the island!"

"So, the map *must* be Shadowmere," suggested Josh.

"Ok," said Harper, "what does that mean?"

"Look at his right arm. He's leaning on a book." Freddie held up the leather-bound one he'd saved from the thief. "It's this very one," he whispered.

"It's almost as if he wanted someone to know," said Leo.

"Perhaps he did," said Noz. "Perhaps it was his last message to the world, and we've decoded it!"

"Come on," urged Josh, "let's see if we can make any sense of the map now we know it *is* Shadowmere."

They trooped downstairs into the dining room.

"Where's the map?" asked Freddie anxiously.

"Did anyone take it with them?" said Josh, a sinking feeling stirring in the pit of his stomach.

"Weasel face!" retorted Josh furiously. "*Ma foi*—my faith, if I get my hands on him…"

"We shouldn't have left it," responded Freddie sadly. "Now we don't know what we're looking for."

"Come on," said Harper soothingly. "Things aren't as bad as you think."

"Oh yes," replied Leo sarcastically. "We've lost the map and have no idea now what to do."

"It's not Harper's fault, Leo," reprimanded Josh. Harper just smiled.

"It's okay," she said, holding up a sheet of paper. "I took this with me when we went upstairs!"

"It's your sketch of the map!" shouted Leo excitedly.

"Oh, well done!" And he hugged her.
"Sorry," he whispered.

Chapter Eight

Grounded Birds

"Right, Leo," said Harper firmly, "as of now, your swimming lessons are being intensified. We've got to get to Shadowmere Island as soon as possible, and you've got to swim to an acceptable standard before we take the boat across. Come on!"

"What, now?" asked Leo.

"Yes, now," she replied.

The two went off to change into their swimwear while the others stayed at the table, discussing recent events.

Jack sprawled out under the table, dog napping. The twins' mum didn't like him in the dining room, but he took full advantage of her not being there.

Freddie spread Harper's sketch out on the table. And he started to chuckle.

The others looked at him in astonishment.

"Whatever are you laughing at?" said Josh.

"I was thinking," he replied, "how the map crumbled when Harper started to unfold it. A whole corner fell apart. Whoever took it, it's probably just dust by now."

The children leant over, looking at the map that Harper had sketched.

"It looks pretty good to me," said Noz. "In fact, more than good. It's amazing!"

"What are these things?" asked Josh. He indicated

the circular shapes with the arrows that Harper had stuck on pointing to them.

SHADOWMERE ISLAND

"Churches?" suggested Noz.

"I wouldn't think there'd be two churches on a tiny island," responded Freddie.

"Hopefully, it will make sense when we get there," said Josh.

"Noz, would you carry on looking through the book?" requested Freddie. "Luckily, I took that upstairs with me, or it would have been taken along with the map."

Noz continued reading, and Josh and Freddie sorted through the pile of papers.

After an hour or so, Noz put the book down.

"I can't see anything in here about the island or Captain Jack," he stated, "and anyway, there's so much writing, it would take me a week to read the lot. Although—" He picked up the book and opened the cover. "There is a verse written on the flyleaf in old-fashioned writing. I looked at it earlier and I wondered what it was all about."

Verily, amidst the grounded Rukhs, Fair Luna hath ceased her consumption at the tithe but doth present Matthew a count of seven secure paths and a tally of thirteen treacherous ways.

"We're back!" Leo and Harper burst into the dining room, still wet from swimming.

Leo was grinning from ear to ear like a Cheshire cat.

"It's going well, then?" said Noz, and Leo nodded happily.

"I'm amazed," said Harper. "I've never known anybody to pick up the basics so quickly. To go from non-swimmer to competent beginner in a few lessons is incredible."

"Well done, Leo," congratulated Freddie. "We are all so proud of you."

"You go off and get changed," said Josh, "because we've found something quite exciting!"

"You'd better put all this away, Freddie," warned Harper. "Your mum's on her way in. We just saw her parking in the lane."

There was a flurry of activity, and the book, the map and all the papers disappeared into the bureau in quick time.

Mrs Dubois looked doubtfully at the children as she came in. "You're quiet," she said.

"Just a bit tired, Mum, after a busy day," replied Josh.

"Hmm," she responded, looking for signs of an adventure in progress. Seeing nothing, she said, "I got some shopping while I was out, so you can all help me bring it in and pack it away. Then it's teatime, so don't go rushing off anywhere." She paused as they were about to leave. "Do you know anything about that tatty old lorry parked in the lane? It looks like the one that almost forced us off the road."

"It's probably that awful weasel man. Perhaps he's a local, and it's broken down?" answered Freddie. "That wouldn't surprise me, seeing the way he drives." He omitted to mention that Noz had lifted his keys from his pocket.

"That's not kind to call the unfortunate man a weasel," reprimanded his mum. "Right, fetch the shopping."

It was collected and packed in the cupboards, and tea was hurriedly eaten. Afterwards, the children hurried to the sitting room, unable to contain their excitement.

"It's a riddle," pointed out Noz, "written in the front of the book. He read it out again for the benefit of Harper and Leo;

Verily, amidst the grounded Rukhs, Fair Luna hath ceased her consumption at the tithe but doth present Matthew a count of seven secure paths and a tally of thirteen treacherous ways.

"That makes no sense at all," responded Leo. "What on earth is a Rukh? And secure paths and treacherous ways?"

"It's a clue, of course," reasoned Harper. "It's not meant to be clear to everyone. That's why it's called cryptic."

"Isn't that your department, Freddie?" asserted Josh. "You and Dad have often written coded messages to each other."

"I'm scratching my head over this one," admitted

Freddie. "So, let's start at the beginning. What is a Rukh?"

"Old English or some other language, perhaps?" responded Noz.

"Dictionary, please, Leo," called out Freddie.

Leo revisited the bookcase, returning with the large volume.

"It makes a change to check these things in a book instead of googling," he stated.

Then he looked up the word under 'Birds' and read aloud;

Rukh—also spelt Roc. A gigantic mythological bird found in Arabian stories said to be able to carry off an elephant or a rhinoceros in its claws.

"We all need to think here," said Freddie. "We'll read out each section, and you can all give your suggestions. Harper, be ready with your paper and pen."

He picked up the book, handing it to Noz. "You found the clue," he said, "so you should have the privilege of reading it to us. Not all at once. Section by section."

Noz took it and read it aloud.

Amidst the grounded Rukhs…

"So, if rukh equals roc, what's a *grounded* roc?" he asked.

"I saw a book about birds when I was searching in the bookcase," said Leo. "I'll fetch it."

He returned with it clutched in his hand. After checking the contents, he said, "There's nothing about grounded birds."

"That's not helpful then," said Josh.

"I've been thinking," responded Freddie. "Do you remember when we flew to Spain on holiday once?"

"I do," responded Josh. "We sat in the plane for hours and hours in the heat because it couldn't take off for some reason that I forget now."

"What did the pilot say?"

"That's it!" said Josh. "He said that our plane had been grounded!"

"So it couldn't fly!" said Harper, quickly seeing where the conversation was going.

"So," said Freddie, "grounded and not flying means the same things. Flightless! Check that book again, Leo, and see if there is anything about flightless birds, especially rocs."

Turning to the section on flightless birds, Leo read through the list.

"There are ostriches, penguins, and chickens, but no mention of rukhs or rocs."

"Perhaps it's not a bird? What other kind of rukh is there?" asked Josh.

"Don't tell me," responded Leo resignedly, "look in the dictionary."

He applied himself to it and, a few moments later, said;

Rukh. An Arabic term for what in English is now called a castle. See chess.

"Oh my goodness, that is so epic," cried out Freddie in exhilaration. "Of course it is." He pointed to the sketch map Harper had drawn.

"Look at these circular marks with crosses that Harper has helpfully marked with arrows. They must be our rukhs or castles."

"So, it's 'amidst' or, in modern English, 'between' the castles that we need to look," enthused Leo.

"I think," said Freddie, "that we've just solved our first clue."

"Okay," said Noz. "Next." He read aloud;

Fair Luna hath ceased her consumption at the tithe.

There was quiet as they all puzzled over possible meanings.

"Josh," called out Freddie, "tell me the meaning of 'Fair Luna.'"

Josh thought for a moment, and then his eyes lit up. "*C'est tres simple*—it's quite easy. Lune is French for the moon, and Luna must be Latin for the same thing, although it has been used as a name too."

"Latin was spoken a lot in the 17th Century," affirmed Noz. "I learned it in a history lesson at school."

"So," said Harper, "Fair Luna is the moon?"

"We think so," replied Freddie.

"Then what's consumption?" asked Josh.

"Leo!" said Harper.

"I know; check the dictionary," he responded obediently. "Ok, this is what it says;"

Consumption. Especially in relation to pulmonary disease.

"It's no clearer," said Freddie. "**Pulmonary**—I know that's to do with the lungs—but I can't see how it fits in with moons and castles, can you?"

"Perhaps I can help," offered Noz. "My mum says that I suffer from excess consumption. I think she means I overeat!"

Leo closed the dictionary and placed it on the table. "All this brainwork has made me quite peckish," Noz announced. "I'll see what your mum brought back from the shops." And with that, he got up and left for the kitchen.

"It's only been a little while since we all ate," responded Harper. "I don't know where Noz puts it all. I'm still feeling full and couldn't eat a thing."

Noz returned shortly afterwards, munching on a chocolate bar.

Freddie stared at him so hard that Noz felt quite self-conscious.

"What's up?" he queried. "Haven't you seen a chap eat before?"

"Harper just said she couldn't eat anything because she felt full. Most people, when full, don't consume any more food," answered Freddie.

"How does that help?" mumbled Noz through his mouthful of confectionery.

"I see!" reasoned Harper excitedly. "The answer to the clue is 'full.' We're talking about the full moon!"

"That's what I thought," replied Freddie. "Luna is full. What have we got now in modern English, Noz?"

Noz quickly swallowed and read from Harper's notes;

Between the castles, when the moon is full.

"No, there's a word before that," said Josh. "What is that word 'tithe?'"

"I know what tithe means," said Noz, taking his glasses off and waving them triumphantly in the air. "It's a word used when people give money in

62

churches. It means ten."

The Six sat silently, full of excitement that the clues written so many hundreds of years ago were making sense.

Harper said, "So, we need to get out to the island when there's a full moon and at ten o'clock at night."

"There aren't that many full moons," replied Josh, who had made a study of stars and planets, "and our holiday finishes at the end of the week, when we have to go home. There are just two days every year during a full moon when the sun rises *exactly* from the east and sets *exactly* west. That might be important."

"We might be too late then," said Noz.

There was a moment of silence, and the spirits of the Secret Six sank.

"Then all this has been for nothing?" asked Harper sadly.

"Before we give up," said Freddie, "let's see when the next full moon is. Who knows, we might still be in with a chance."

"There's a calendar on the kitchen wall," reported Harper. "It has all kinds of information about things such as Easter and Bank Holidays. It might have a bit about full moons."

She hurried off to check, returning with the calendar in her hand.

"What's the date today?" she asked.

Noz looked at his watch. "It's the 21st," he answered. Harper wiped her eyes, and Leo jumped up to comfort her.

Jack, in his usual way, padded up to her and leaned

his weight against her legs. She reached down and stroked his ears, and he rolled onto his back to have his underneath tickled.

"It's okay," Leo consoled her, "we've done our best." She handed the calendar to him, too emotional to speak.

"It's not that. Look," she announced, her voice strangely husky.

"Oh my," declared Leo. "There's a full moon on the 22nd, which is tomorrow!"

There was a shocked silence for a moment, and then the children burst into cheers of joy.

"We're not too late!" cried Harper. "The Secret Six can still solve the mystery!"

The loud celebrations caused the twins' mum to hurry in.

"What's going on?" she asked. "Why all the noise?"

"We've just found out there's a full moon tomorrow, Mum," said Josh. "And we think we'll get a really good view of it from here."

"I've never known either you or Freddie to be interested in moons," she said as she went out, shaking her head in disbelief.

Freddie got up and discreetly closed the door behind her.

"We'd better get a move on," he said. "We have to solve the last clue, and then tomorrow, get the boat ready and sail."

He looked towards Leo. "Do you think you'll be okay so soon?"

Leo looked at Harper for encouragement, and she nodded.

"He'll be just fine," she said, "and anyway, there's a

lifejacket in the boat if we need it."

"So we're down to the last clue," stated Noz. "Shall I read it out?"

"Good idea," responded Freddie, "then we can all put our brains into solving it."

Noz opened the book and read;

...but doth present Matthew, a count of seven secure paths and a tally of thirteen treacherous ways.

"Anyone?" asked Freddie, hopefully.

"That's a hard one," responded Josh. "And it sounds like an awful lot of paths. Seven safe ones but thirteen dangerous ones!"

"Does anyone know a Matthew?" asked Leo.

But despite thinking hard until their brains hurt, none of them could come up with any ideas.

"I think I know," said Josh.

"The answer?" replied Freddie in disbelief.

Josh shook his head. "I'm not that bright, but I know someone who is. Someone who does crossword puzzles!"

He jumped up from the table and went into the hallway. "Mum!" he shouted, "where are you?"

"Poor old Mum," he said on returning to the dining room, "she's getting really confused and wondering why we've suddenly started doing crosswords and checking out moons!"

"What did she say?" said Freddie urgently.

"I said we had a hard crossword clue."

"And..?" asked Leo.

"She said it was probably a Bible verse. Matthew chapter seven, verse thirteen."

"And?" responded Harper.

"And she said we needed to look it up ourselves. She said it would do us good!"

"Back to the bookshelf, Leo," said Freddie. "This time, see if you can find a Bible."

Leo hurried off and returned, carrying an enormous book under his arm.

"This, believe it or not, is a Bible," he said, heaving it onto the table before them. "It's pretty ancient, like the map we found."

"Matthew, anyone?" asked Noz.

Nobody knew. The exact whereabouts within the huge volume was a mystery.

"There must be a list of contents at the front," said Freddie.

Leo ran his finger down the page. "Here we are," he announced, "it's towards the back."

He carefully turned the tissue-like pages until he found the Book of Matthew.

"I can't understand the numbers," he protested. "They're all XX and XV!"

"They're Roman numerals," explained Noz. "I learned them—"

"You learned them in history at school!" shouted the rest of the Secret Six.

Noz laughed.

"So, wise one, what is seven and thirteen?" asked Leo.

"Seven is a 'V' followed by 'II,'" responded Noz. "Look, I'll write them down." He picked up a scrap of paper and wrote on the bottom, 'VII.'

"Here we are, Matthew chapter seven," said Leo. "And thirteen?"

'XIII,' wrote Noz.

"This is it," replied Leo. "Matthew chapter seven, verse thirteen."

He read aloud from the page;

Enter in at the narrow gate: for it is the wide gate and broad way that leadeth to destruction: and many there be which go in thereat.

"That sounds worrying," cautioned Harper. "Does this mean we must choose a narrow path or entrance when we get to the spot between the castles? And I don't like the mention of destruction!"

"It sounds like it," responded Josh, "but don't worry, I'm sure all will become clear when we get there. We'll be quite safe if we stay together."

"Noz," said Freddie, "can you read the full translated verse for us?"

Noz once again took Harper's notes. "I don't know why I'm reading this," he said, "when you've done all the writing."

Between the castles, when the moon is full at ten, take the narrow and safe way.

"Does that sound about right?" he asked.

Just then, the twins' mother called out from the landing. "Right, my dears, time for bed. You must be worn out after all your brainwork today. Goodness me, history, crosswords, moons—whatever next!" And so off to bed they went, tired but exhilarated. The 22nd was almost upon them, and they had much to do to prepare for the next part of their adventure. "Can I ask you something?" said Freddie, pausing at the top of the stairs.

"I thought you might," said his mother. "I always know when something is up."

"We would like to visit an island," he told her, recounting the conversation with the fisherman on the beach about using *Swiftwater*. He left out the details of ghosts and treasure and weasels.

"I wish I could check with Dad," she said, "but I can't get hold of him at the moment. He's working on something important, and I mustn't disturb him."

"I think he'd be okay with it," responded Freddie. "We've done lots of sailing with him, and he knows we're competent and safe."

"You're probably right," answered his mother, "but all the same, I worry about you children. Whatever happened to the crossword puzzles, history searches and moons? I thought for a while that you were settling down to something quiet and educational for once!"

Freddie squeezed her and smiled adoringly. "Thanks, Mum," he said and hurried off to bed.

"By the way, we might camp on the island overnight to see the full moon," he shouted, and he disappeared into his room before Mrs Dubois had a chance to disagree.

"I'll be along in a minute to kiss you boys goodnight," she shouted along the landing, chuckling to herself, knowing it would embarrass them.

"Mum!" replied Freddie and Josh in unison, "we *are* twelve years old now."

Chapter Nine

Setting Sail

The following morning, after breakfast, the children could hardly wait to begin preparations for their voyage to Shadowmere Island.

"Have we got everything?" asked Josh.

"Here's the map and the chart," replied Harper. "We'll need the map when we land on Shadowmere."

"And we need to check our course to the island," responded Freddie.

"We'd better do that now," said Josh, "before we get underway."

The children crowded into the dining room and spread the chart on the table.

69

"It looks fairly straightforward from here to there," said Freddie. "Some submerged rocks and shallows are marked to avoid as we get near the island—they're the skull and crossbones drawings."

"They look a bit scary," said Leo.

"It's just a warning," replied Freddie. "If you look, there's a dotted line charting a course between the dangerous rocks and shallows."

Josh considered it for a few minutes. "We must line up the castle with the triangle mark. We know about the castle, but I'm unsure about the triangle, considering this was drawn a long time ago. It's a marker of some sort. I just hope it's still there."

"It'll be awkward if it's gone," said Noz.

"We have to find a safe place to beach the boat. It looks rocky—a natural fortress. We don't want to wreck *Swiftwater*," emphasised Josh.

"Okay. To the boat," commanded Freddie, "and make sure you've got your camping equipment. If things work out okay, we'll stay on the island for the night."

"Give me a few minutes," said Harper, "and I'll join you on the beach. There's something I want to do first."

She picked up the chart and the map before hurrying away.

The excited children looked at her curiously, but they went down to the beach, carrying tents, sleeping bags, food, bottles of fresh water and the other necessities needed for an overnight camp.

Freddie also carried Jack and was relieved when he finally got to the beach. "You're getting heavy, Jack," he declared.

The dog wagged his tail and trotted off to sniff around the rocks.

"Before we set sail, Leo, it's more swimming practice, I'm afraid." He looked around just as Harper ran down the steps. "Is that okay with you, Harper?" he said.

"Of course. Come on, Leo," she insisted, "let's go. It will be worth it when we head out on the water."

She thrust the map and chart into Freddie's hand. "Here, look after these."

Josh pulled the tarp cover off the little craft, folded it, and stowed it in the bow.

"Okay, Noz," said Freddie, "let's check our boat out. First, we have to check she's seaworthy."

He leant forward, looking inside. "These little boats have a bung," he said. "It's to drain any water that may be inside. We don't want the *Mere* coming in, so the first thing to do is ensure the bung has been replaced since the boat was last used."

Jack jumped into the boat, excited by all the surrounding action, and sat down in the bow as if waiting for it to be launched.

"Just as well we checked," declared Noz, holding up a bright blue rubber plug before pushing it hard into the drain hole. "We'd very likely have sunk otherwise!"

"It's best to get everything ready before it goes in the water," instructed Josh. "The boat is much more stable on dry land."

"That makes sense," answered Noz, "so what do we do now?"

"Let's look at the sail," responded Freddie. "We'll

unfurl it from the boom and make sure it has no holes in it."

"Unfurl? Boom? What is this strange language?" queried Noz. "We used to hire boats with engines when we went on holiday. They're a lot easier!"

Freddie laughed. "But not as much fun. Unfurl is just a boating term for unwrapping the sail. The boom is this horizontal spar extending from the mast to which the bottom of the mainsail is attached. This line—" he held it up, "is called a sheet, used to let the sail out or bring it in, depending on the wind. Don't get confused because a sheet isn't a sail. But don't worry; Josh will take care of all that."

He pointed to the front of the boat. "We also use the name bow for the boat's front end and stern for the back. That's about all you need to know for now."

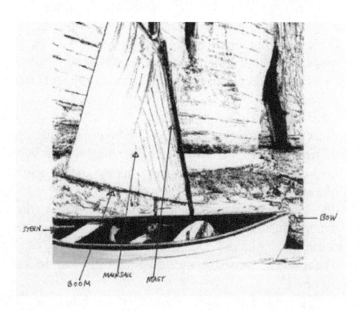

Josh hauled on the **halyard**, and the mainsail rose and filled, flapping vigorously in the onshore breeze. "That looks good," declared Freddie. "No holes in it and a gentle little breeze to get us underway." He went to the stern. "Give me a hand with the rudder," he said. "This is the bit that sits in the water and changes our course when I move the **tiller**, so we have to lift it out of the way before moving the boat along the beach."

So, the rudder was lifted, and *Swiftwater* was ready to set sail to the mysterious island they longed to explore.

"If we have trouble with the sail, there's a pair of oars," pointed out Noz.

"Brilliant," responded Josh. "After a bit of practice, we should manage just fine. And we might need the oars when we get to our mooring. It's difficult to navigate narrow waters under sail."

Harper and Leo, fresh from swimming practice, joined them.

"That looks amazing!" enthused Harper. "I can't wait to try it out."

Leo looked apprehensive.

"Isn't it risky?" he said. When it was just talk, he'd felt okay with the prospect of sailing off on an adventure, but now confronted with the reality of the boat in front of him, his courage began to fail.

"It will be fine," said Freddie. "I remember my dad giving this advice." He screwed up his face in concentration.

Pride says it's impossible
Experience says it's risky

Reason says it's pointless
Our hearts whisper, give it a try.

The children nodded their heads in agreement.

"Your dad was right," said Harper. "Let's give it a try."

"That's exactly what an adventure should be about," voiced Josh.

"There's just one last thing before we go," said Freddie seriously.

"Harper, despite encouraging us to be adventurous, my dad trusts Josh and me to be sensible and not stupid. To do the right thing as best we can. So it's your decision whether Leo is competent enough at swimming to travel in the boat. If you say no, then we don't go. It's all of us or none of us, remember?"

Harper looked steadily at her brother. He stared at the ground, suddenly unsure of what she might say.

But she smiled broadly. "He will be absolutely fine," she replied, much to everyone's relief.

Then, with the five alternatively pushing and pulling, they soon had the boat, stern first, in the water. Jack remained in the bow, enjoying the ride.

"Hold on, me hearties!"

It was the twins' mum. In all the activity, she had climbed unnoticed down the steps and was standing on the beach, watching them.

"Mum? What's up?" enquired Freddie.

"Nothing at all," she responded, "Not if you know what you are doing. But if you thought I would allow you to sail off with no checks, you are mistaken."

"Oh," said Josh and Freddie together.

"Oh, indeed," said their mother. She looked across the water. "If you are going to make the best of the

tide and this breeze, you must get your skates on."
"What do you want us to do?" asked Freddie
hesitantly.

"First of all," she responded, "I know you two can
swim, but what about the others? I can't allow this
little escapade unless all the boat's crew can swim."
She pointed to a rock in the distance.

"I want to see you all swim to that rock and back!"
The children looked at Leo nervously. They all
trusted that, as Harper had confirmed he could swim,
then he could. Thank goodness they had been
sensible enough to make him take swimming
lessons! But they were not so sure how he would
cope under the eagle eye of Mrs Dubois.

They needn't have worried. Leo was first into the
water, striking out for the rock. There was too much
energetic splashing, and his enthusiasm didn't
correspond with the speed at which he moved
forward, which was relatively slow. But he *was*
moving and swimming, which was the important
thing.

Then they laughed because Jack jumped in and
swiftly paddled after him.

"And the rest of you?" said Mrs Dubois.

In a matter of minutes, the Secret Six were in the
water, and in no time at all, the rock had been
navigated, and they were back on the beach.

"Very well done, Leo," whispered Harper.

"Is that it?" asked Freddie hopefully.

"Not quite," replied his mum. "I want to see your
seamanship and how you manage *Swiftwater.* Off
you go!"

"Hold this!" Freddie threw a rope attached to the bow of the boat at Josh.

"The technical name for this is a **painter**," he explained to Noz, Leo and Harper. "It's to tie it so it won't drift off."

Then he jumped aboard, sitting in the stern and taking charge of the tiller. "Take your time getting aboard," he instructed the others, "and distribute yourselves in the boat to equal the weight. Don't all sit on one side, or we'll tip over!"

Mrs Dubois watched approvingly as Josh stayed on the beach, holding the painter while the others climbed aboard, one by one.

"Here, Leo," directed Freddie, "you sit in the bow with the anchor, as you're the smallest and lightest, and take charge of Jack. We don't want him leaping overboard for a swim!" He grinned. "You can be our ship's boy."

"You'd better be the captain then," advised Josh. "We need someone in charge when out on the water."

"I'm okay with that," replied Freddie. "You be the first mate, as you're the only other with any real experience. Harper, Noz. I hope you don't mind, but you must be crew as you've no sailing experience."

Once satisfied that all were safely in, First Mate Josh pushed *Swiftwater* into the water and pulled himself over the stern. Then he coiled the painter neatly before positioning himself on the **port** side, taking charge of the sheet controlling the mainsail.

"One thing you need to be aware of," warned Freddie. "When we turn, we will gybe. That means the boom will swing across in the wind, bringing the sail with it. You must keep your head down then, or it will hit you, which would be painful. And you could be knocked overboard, which is extremely dangerous if you are knocked unconscious. We don't want to mess this up, especially when Mum is watching!"

Noz wedged himself alongside the main thwart below the **gunwale**. "I think I'll stay put here," he exclaimed. "It seems safer than having my head knocked off!"

"Captain Freddie will call 'ready about,' and when that happens, be alert, duck, and all will be well," instructed Josh.

"Stand by," shouted Freddie, his voice brimming with exhilaration as Josh heaved on the halyard to raise the mainsail. It filled with the wind as Freddie set *Swiftwater* on course for the island, and Josh pulled it in with the sheet until it was taut. After about a hundred metres, they went about, heading back to shore.

"Ready about!" shouted Freddie, and the crew ducked as the boom flew across, taking the wind-filled sail with it.

"Well done!" he exclaimed as he set their course back to his mother, who was watching intently from the beach.

With the boat heading into the wind, they had to **tack** back and forth half a dozen times to progress back to land.

As they approached, Josh lowered the mainsail in good time, and the boat had enough way for Freddie to steer it the last few metres, gently nosing into the shore to nestle against the sand.

Josh threw the painter to his mum, who caught it capably and held the boat fast.

"That was very well done, all of you," she exclaimed. "I can see you will be safe with your captain and first mate."

Freddie leapt ashore and hugged his mother. "Thanks, Mum," he said, "you're the best!"

"Flattery will get you nowhere," she said. "Here, you'll need this." She handed over a wicker basket with a cloth secured around it. "It's food, so keep an eye on Noz!"

Harper took it for safekeeping, and they all laughed, including Noz.

"I *am* hungry," he said plaintively.

"And this is for you, too." She passed Freddie a square of cloth attached to a wooden spar. "You might want to run this up the mast. It will help you gauge the wind's direction and identify your boat. I made it for you last night."

He was overwhelmed. "Mum, that is so epic! More than that. Super epic!"

He turned to the rest of the crew. "It's a flag. Look!" It was a white cloth with the number six in Roman numerals emblazoned in black. Underneath was the name: *Swiftwater.*

"It's got the number six for the Secret Six," whispered Harper.

"First Mate," said Freddie, "run up the flag!"

"Aye, Aye, Captain," Josh replied as he attached the flagstaff to the line, and soon, the little pennant fluttered proudly atop the mast in the breeze. He pushed the boat back into the deep water and leapt aboard, coiling the painter in the stern before hauling up the mainsail.

It unfurled like a magnificent banner as the wind filled it. With a gentle thrust from the playful breeze, the boat glided away from the safety of the shore, venturing bravely into the vast expanse of the water, carrying aboard five adventurous children and their trusty four-legged friend.

Leo settled down in the bow, holding onto Jack, who was keenly sniffing the air. Noz remained reclining between the thwarts while Harper sat on the **starboard** side. Josh sat to port, managing the sheet and the lines that raised and lowered the sail. Freddie put the tiller down, setting an easterly course away from land.

Mrs Dubois remained, watching them from the shore.

"*Bon Voyage,*" she shouted, waving furiously at the departing vessel. "*Bon Voyage!*"

The captain and crew waved back energetically as the craft creamed through the water and moved silently away.

"*Adieu, Mama, adieu!*" shouted Freddie and Josh.

"Goodbye!" called out the rest of the Six.

Jack gave a joyful bark, roused by all the eager shouting.

"Go *Swiftwater!*" cried Leo, and as if in response, the boat surged forward, leaving a trail of foaming water bubbling in its wake.

Chapter Ten

Onwards, Swiftwater!

Freddie handed the chart and the map to Harper.
"It seemed bare," she explained, "so I inked in

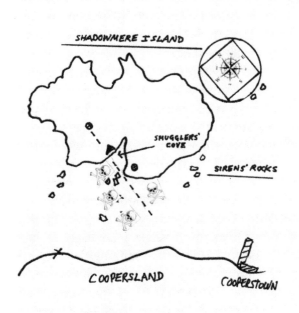

a few names to enhance it."
Freddie leaned in, curiosity twinkling in his eyes.
"Coopersland?" he inquired, pointing to the marked
area on the chart. "Cooperstown?"
Harper nodded. "Yes. We know that the original

81

owner of Swiftwater Cottage—the man who disappeared—was named William Cooper. I thought the poor man needed to be remembered. I've inked in the town's name along the coast and called it Cooperstown, and also drew in the public jetty in case we visit."

"For those who don't know," explained Freddie, "a jetty is a wooden platform where boats dock."

A smile played on Josh's lips as he looked at the names on the chart. "I like that," he responded, and Noz and Leo eagerly agreed.

Freddie's gaze shifted to a bold 'X' marked on the border of Coopersland. "What does the 'X' on the border indicate?" he asked.

"That's where we launched Swiftwater from," Harper replied. "And I thought Smugglers' Cove—" she pointed to the cove on the island — "was a good name for our mooring. I named it after the bay in Cornwall, where we had our first adventure with dear old Aunt Beehive." [1]

Excitement filled the air as Harper pointed to a cluster of rocks south of the island. "I named those 'Sirens' Rocks,'" she declared. They reminded me of the Sirens in Greek mythology who used to lure sailors onto the rocks with their singing so that they wrecked their boats."

Freddie beamed with pride. "Well done, Harper!"

Noz chuckled. "I think the sailors used to put cheese in their ears so they didn't hear them," he said with a grin. "I think I learned that in a lesson—"

The others didn't allow him time to finish.

"You learned it in a lesson at school!" they shouted

[1] The Adventure at Smugglers' Cove

gleefully.

Noz grinned good-naturedly. "You've remembered," he responded.

Freddie turned to Leo and called out.

"Ships Boy, if you hear any Sirens, call out at once!" Leo saluted, his eyes scanning the horizon intently. "Aye, Aye, Captain," he replied dutifully, ready to alert them immediately if any singing was heard.

Once the boat had ventured away from the shore, Freddie adjusted the **helm** to port, guiding their vessel along the coastline to the south. He had noticed several large passenger boats ferrying sightseers up and down the *Mere* in the deep-water channel.

"As Harper suggested, why don't we pay a visit to Cooperstown?" said Freddie. He looked up at the pennant his mother had made, flying gallantly in the breeze. "It's a straight run, and it'll give us some practice in sailing *Swiftwater* and seeing how she handles before making the journey to the island with its navigation hazards."

"That's a great idea," agreed Josh. "We can see how the natives live!"

"Perhaps we can go ashore and get some supplies," said Noz. "I'm not sure if we packed enough treats." The others just smiled. There they were, together in a magnificent boat, heading for an unexplored island and the prospect of solving the centuries-long mystery of William Cooper and Captain Jack's will, and all Noz could think about was his stomach.

As *Swiftwater* was **running before the wind**, there was no need to tack, and they made fast progress, their little craft cutting through the water with ease.

"Leo," called out Freddie.

"Captain?" he responded.

"Keep a weather eye open for sight of land on the starboard side, and a safe harbour."

"Aye, aye," answered Leo, scanning ahead with the binoculars.

Harper hung her arm over the side of the boat, letting her fingers trail through the fast-moving water. It was warm from the morning's heat, giving her a pleasurable, calming feeling.

"This is perfect," she announced. "I've never been in a boat before, and for the six of us to venture out on the water together like this is something I never dreamed would be possible."

"It's only possible because you taught me to swim," responded Leo, "otherwise we wouldn't be out here all alone, with no adults and an adventure just over the horizon."

Harper smiled and closed her eyes, reflecting on the vastness of the water and the excitement of the voyage they were undertaking as the Secret Six.

"I learned a poem once," she said. "I hope I've got it right."

The boys screwed up their faces. Poetry wasn't their thing.

I must go down to the seas again, to the lonely sea and the sky,
And all I ask is a tall ship and a star to steer her by.
And the wheel's kick and the wind's song and the white sail's shaking,
And a grey mist on the sea's face, and a grey dawn breaking.

Her voice faded, and there was silence, except for the cries of the wheeling gulls above, the crackle of the sail stretching taut in the wind, and the rhythmic sound of the water slapping against the hull.

Onwards *Swiftwater!*

Sail on little boat, to uncharted territories, hidden coves, unknown islands and adventure.

Chapter Eleven

Cooperstown

"Land ahoy!" shouted Leo. "Land ahoy!"

And there it was. The town's public mooring just off the starboard bow. It was busy with craft of various sizes, both sail and motor, tied up in a neat line.

"There's a space right at the end," sang out First Mate Josh.

"I see it," replied Captain Freddie. "Stand by to lower the mainsail."

"Ship's Boy!"

"Captain?"

"Take hold of the painter and jump ashore as soon as we dock. Tie it off against one of the **cleats**."

"Aye, aye," responded Leo, crouching on his haunches and ready to spring ashore at the right moment. He wasn't exactly sure what a cleat was, but he knew that the line he was holding was the painter that Freddie had spoken about earlier, and there was sure to be something to tie it to when he got ashore. As they closed with the wooden jetty, a group of curious people stood watching, and for the first time, Freddie felt nervous.

What if he messed up? What if he missed the jetty or, even worse, collided with it?

Almost as if he'd read his twin's mind, Josh caught his eye and smiled encouragingly.

"You know you can do it, Captain Freddie," he said

encouragingly. "You've moored a dinghy a thousand times before, and you know what needs to be done."

Freddie nodded. "Thanks," he mouthed.

The wind had dropped to a gentle breeze, so he kept the sail up until almost the last moment.

"Lower the mainsail!"

Josh released the **downhaul** line and down came the sail. Leaning forward, he grabbed it in big handfuls, reefed it around the boom, and tied it off with small lines.

There was just enough way on *Swiftwater* to allow it to glide in, its bow gently touching the jetty. Freddie put the tiller hard to port, Josh slid an oar into the port side oarlock, pushed forward, and the stern of the little boat swung perfectly in until it was **parallel** with the jetty.

Then Freddie and Leo stepped neatly ashore, the captain with the stern line and Leo with the painter, tying them off in figure of eight knots around the cleats provided.

"Phew!" exhaled Freddie, and the audience watching clapped politely.

"Well done, youngsters," exclaimed a man wearing a yachting association cap, "I couldn't have done it better myself."

Freddie waved in acknowledgement, sailor to sailor. "Good job, crew," he said. And he beamed happily.

"Someone needs to stay with the boat," he said, "certainly after the weasel tried to steal our guidebook to Captain Jack's treasure!"

"Shh," cautioned Harper. "You never know who's listening."

"Leave it to me," volunteered Leo. "I'll stay put and

keep a weather eye out for any pirates."

The crew went ashore, with Jack going first. He had this unique ability to get to the front of the queue.

Leo sat on the side of the jetty, dangling his legs over the side. It was a sunny morning, and the glint of the sun on the water and the smell of boats and boating was **intoxicating**.

Shrouds rattled with a tinny ringing sound against aluminium masts on the bigger sailing boats. The odour of diesel from outboard motors chugging their path across the bay wafted in the air as the water gurgled underneath his legs, swashing and swirling around the **stanchions** supporting the jetty. The cries of the gulls overhead resonated in the warmth of the day, ranging from high-pitched squawks to plaintive wails across land, water and sky.

He hadn't meant to. He took his responsibility as protector of *Swiftwater* seriously.

But the warmth of the sun and the hypnotic sounds around him had a dramatic and unexpected effect.

He fell asleep.

✳✳✳

"Leo! Leo!"

Freddie's urgent shouting caused Leo to awake with a start.

"What have you done?" asked Freddie angrily.

"What?" It took a moment for him to come to his senses.

"How could you? You've been sleeping on watch. *Swiftwater* is gone!"

The awful reality hit Leo like a hammer blow, and

his heart sank. He leapt to his feet, shaking his **befuddled** head, and it was true. An empty berth was on the jetty where their little boat had been tied.

He frantically scanned the waterway in all directions. But to no avail. Their boat was nowhere to be seen.

Chapter Twelve

Windchaser

"We won't talk about this now," said Freddie sharply. "The important thing at the moment is to find out what has happened to *Swiftwater.*" He called the others over. "Josh, you ask around the other boat owners on the jetty and find out if anyone saw anything."

"Aye, aye, captain." Josh looked sadly at Leo, seeing how much he was hurting, but trotted off on his mission as requested.

"Harper, you have a wander around Cooperstown and ask some questions. See if anyone knows anything."

She nodded, too upset to respond, and went off along the water's edge.

"Leo, you report this at the police station. They might have an idea who would steal a boat."

"Aye, aye," he responded and walked dejectedly away.

Jack sat quietly on the jetty's edge, unsure of what was happening but aware that his children were sad about something. He looked at Leo, retreating into the distance before dashing off after Harper.

"Okay, Noz," said Freddie after reflecting for a moment. "You stay here in case any witnesses come by. I'm going to catch up with Leo. I was too hard on him and must put things right."

Some time passed, and Josh returned to the jetty where Noz was waiting.

"Nothing," he said. "I asked all the boat owners, and no one saw *Swiftwater* sail off."

"Surely someone must have seen something?" said Noz.

Josh shrugged. "Apparently not."

"Anything?" Freddie was back from Cooperstown, accompanied by Leo.

The boys shook their heads miserably.

"Where's Harper? And Jack?" said Josh. "Don't say we've lost them too?"

"I think I see her," said Freddie. "And Jack's with her."

The other three boys looked around. "Where? I can't see anything."

"That's because you're looking in the wrong direction," replied Freddie. "Out there, on the water. They're with a ginger-haired girl in a sailing boat. I can't see the name; it's too far off."

They saw the girl at the helm as the boat approached the jetty. She was about the same age as Harper, wearing a white T-shirt with blue hoops on it, shorts, and a red woollen hat pushed jauntily to the back of her head.

"It's named *Windchaser*," observed Freddie as the gap between them closed and the pennant fluttering at their masthead became visible.

"What are Harper and Jack doing aboard?" said Noz in surprise.

"I've no idea," responded Josh. "Perhaps she's enlisted them to search for our boat. I wonder if they need help to tie up?"

Freddie went to the edge of the jetty. "Hello, *Windchaser*," he hollered, "do you want any assistance to dock?"

Jack wagged his tail, and the girl in the hat waved as she released the halyard, dropping the mainsail. As the boat lost its momentum, she put the helm hard over at the last moment. The bow bumped softly against the jetty, and the stern swung in to nestle against the mooring platform.

Before Freddie or Josh could move a muscle, she jumped ashore and tied the stern line to its cleat.

Then, walking calmly to the bow, Harper threw her the painter, which she effortlessly tied off on the jetty. Jack jumped ashore, followed by Harper, who was smiling hugely.

"This is the captain of the *Windchaser*," she said.

"What's going on?" said Josh. "Who is she, and what are you doing on her boat?"

"I *can* answer for myself," said the girl in the hat, looking steadily at the twins with an unflinching gaze. "I'm Summer, and this is my twin, Scarlett."

Freddie looked into the boat. "Twin? There's no one else aboard," he said.

Harper suppressed a laugh as Summer waved her hand in the direction she had just sailed from.

"You're right, whoever you are," she said. "My sister is in that boat!"

A close-hauled sailing boat with a deep-red sail was approaching them. At the tiller was a girl identical to Summer, even down to her clothes. The one difference was that she wasn't wearing a hat.

"It's *Swiftwater!*" gasped Josh. "She's at the helm of

our boat!"

✳✳✳

Jamie 'The Weasel' Jenkins was slouching and talking to another man at the quayside. They were watching *Swiftwater* making its way to the jetty.

"Do you know who they are?" the man asked. Unlike Jenkins, he was dressed smartly in brown corduroy trousers and a tweed jacket, but his clothing didn't hide the fact that he was untrustworthy.

He was Bartholomew Worthington, and although adopting a pretence of old-world charm and **sophistication**, behind the **charade**, all was just deception and greed.

He was known to the police and other criminals in the underworld as 'Black Bart,' after the infamous pirate captain, something he was secretly proud of. Jamie Jenkins shook his head. "The twin girls are a well-known presence in the local community and they are always out on the water in their boat. I caught them on the island once or twice and frightened them off. They're harmless and have no idea what's going on. The other kids turned up a few days ago and are staying at Swiftwater Cottage. Probably holidaymakers."

"I thought that the owner had gone abroad," said Black Bart in irritation, "and we had the place to ourselves?"

"So did I," said the other. "I did manage to look round but was disturbed and had to get out quick!" He omitted to mention that he'd ended up on the floor after tackling Freddie.

"Did you see the book?"

The weasel paused, reluctant to admit he'd held it in his hands. "The kids have it," he said. "I got the map, but it fell to bits."

He took an envelope out of his shoulder bag and handed over the fragments of old paper.

"You idiot," said Black Bart angrily, "the whole thing has just crumbled to dust! Why couldn't you be more careful with such a document?"

Jamie Jenkins **cowed** back as he nervously replied. "I did my best, but I was rumbled and had to make myself scarce."

"This is no use to us at all. We need the book. And *you* need to get it! There's money in this for you if I get the island, remember?"

He did remember. That's all he thought about. Money. Jewels perhaps? Riches beyond his wildest dreams.

"I'll get it," he replied craftily as he watched little Jack running around happily on the jetty, "and I think I know just how to do it."

Chapter Thirteen

Ship's Articles

Swiftwater was safely tied up on the jetty alongside *Windchaser* after being expertly moored by Scarlett. Nevertheless, Leo was furious as he confronted her. "How dare you take our boat!" he shouted. "We thought it had been stolen."

"It was stolen," responded Josh. "You had no right to take it. We've reported it to the police."

At the mention of the police, Scarlett looked anxiously at her sister.

"I thought you needed to be taught a lesson," she responded. "Summer and I have been watching you all, and to sleep on watch is a serious crime at sea. You would have been locked up in the **Brig** for a month in the old days!"

"In case it's escaped your notice," said Josh **irately**, "we aren't at sea; it's not the old days, and we don't have a Brig!"

"You really shouldn't have slept on watch," said Summer.

"Don't keep saying that," said Leo. "I only dozed off for a short while. And I've never done that before!"

"Shall we call a truce?" suggested Harper diplomatically, seeing that things were beginning to **escalate**.

"Can we at least sit down?" enquired Summer, "and do your friends have names?"

Harper looked at Freddie. "Truce?" she said.

He nodded, grudgingly respecting the girls for their handling of the boats. They obviously knew a thing or two about sailing.

They sat in a line along the jetty, and Jack squeezed in between Harper and Summer—that annoyed Leo. Jack was usually a good judge of character, and he didn't like it that their dog had cosied up to the sister of a boat thief.

Freddie was the first to speak.

"I'm Freddie," he said, "and captain of the *Swiftwater*. My twin is the first mate. His name is Josh."

"I'm Noz," responded Noz, "and I'm crew."

"We've already introduced ourselves," said Harper to the girls, "but this is my brother, Leo. He's the ship's boy."

"As is obvious," said Summer, "this is my sister, Scarlett, the first mate of *Windchaser*, and I'm Summer, captain of the vessel."

Freddie thrust his hand forward. "Shall we shake?" he said, "to show there are no hard feelings?"

"We wouldn't usually," responded Scarlett. "We don't have much to do with holidaymakers. They're too much trouble." She smiled at Harper. "But we'll make an exception, as these are your friends."

"And you did a jolly good job of mooring yourself," said Summer to Freddie, who, despite himself, glowed with pleasure. "We were watching you, expecting the usual mess tourists make of it."

She spat on her hand and extended it to him. "It's what seafarers do," she explained, seeing his puzzled expression.

And so they all shared in the ceremony, even Leo, although reluctantly, and the truce began.

"You said you had been watching us?" questioned Harper. "Why is that?"

"You're staying at Captain Jack's place, aren't you?" queried Scarlett, "with your mum and your friends."

"We are," said Noz. "With Freddie and Josh's mum. You seem to know a lot about us, but we know nothing about you."

"There's not a lot to tell," said Summer. "We've lived here all our lives and spend most of our time at sea."

"We call it the sea," said Scarlett, "but it's the *Mere*, really." She grinned in a friendly way. "The sea sounds much more exciting!"

"It does," said Leo. "We are hoping to have an adventure."

"Leo," said Josh, "We don't have to tell them anything!"

"I only said we wanted an adventure," said Leo. "That's all."

"You won't find one around here," replied Summer with a **wry** grin. "It's absolutely dead so far as excitement is concerned."

"What about Shadowmere Island?" asked Leo. "That looks as though it has a few mysteries waiting to be explored." Despite still feeling angry with the girls, he couldn't help but respond to their easy manner.

"Leo!" said Josh. "We don't know who these girls are, so perhaps you shouldn't say too much."

Summer and Scarlett exchanged worried glances.

"You keep away from there," said Scarlett defensively.

"It's not as if anyone owns it," retorted Noz, forgetting the warning to Leo. "Not until it's sold, anyway."

"Yes, someone does own it," said Summer fiercely, "and it's not for sale!"

"Why are you so angry?" asked Harper gently. "What is it about this island that causes so much fighting?"

Scarlett and Summer exchanged one of those mysterious, unspoken thoughts that only twins have.

"I agree," said Summer. "The boys don't seem too friendly, but I trust Harper."

"Would they keep it to themselves?" asked Scarlett.

"Let's find out," responded Summer.

"Are you having a secret conversation?" asked Leo.

"It's a twins thing," said Freddie. "Josh and I do it all the time."

Summer turned to the Six. "You'll have to sign our ship's articles before we can tell you anything."

Freddie exchanged looks with his crew. "Are you happy to leave this to me?" he asked.

"Let's see what we're signing first," responded Harper cautiously, "before we agree to anything."

And the rest of the Secret Six were of the same mind.

"First Mate," said Summer, "fetch them."

"Aye, Captain," responded Scarlett. She went aboard *Windchaser,* returning with a black tin box that had been stowed under the forward thwarts.

She handed it to Summer, who took a sheet of paper from inside and read;

Ahoy, mateys! These are the articles of the pirate code and the consequences that await those who dare to break it.

100

"*We* aren't pirates," interrupted Leo. "If anyone's a pirate, it's your sister!"

"We wrote this for *Windchaser*," said Scarlett, ignoring the comment, "but if you aren't happy…"

She took a pencil, crossed out 'pirate' and inserted 'buccaneer.'

"What's a buccaneer?" queried Josh.

"An adventurer," answered Noz, "I learnt about them—"

"In a history lesson at school!" chimed in the entire crew of *Swiftwater.*

"Don't worry," said Harper to the twin girls, "You'll find out what that's all about if you are around us long enough!"

Summer continued reading her document.

The Birth of the Code
When the oceans were ruled by great ships and daring adventurers, buccaneers realised the need for order and drafted their own rules. They were known as the pirate's code or ship's articles.

1. Discipline on the Open Sea
This code is vital for maintaining order on the tumultuous waves. Guidelines are laid out within its pages to keep the crew in line. From how to address the captain to the sharing of treasure. Every pirate must know their responsibilities and the consequences of disobedience.

2. Sharing the Treasure
Treasure must be divided fairly among the crew. The code dictates how the treasure will be shared, preventing quarrels and promoting unity. This will

forge a bond of camaraderie amidst the perilous life
of a buccaneer.

3. The Price for Disobedience
The code isn't to be taken lightly. Any swashbuckler
who dares to break these sacred rules will face dire
consequences from being **marooned** *on a deserted*
island, to death!

"Just a few points, Summer," said Freddie.

"Okay," she responded.

"Your ship's articles mention only one captain. It
needs to be amended to show there are two."

Summer glanced at Scarlett. "Fair enough," she said
and amended the document with her pencil.

"Anything else?"

"We need to be clear on what the responsibilities
are."

"That's easy," said Scarlett. "Obey the captains, no
slacking, share any treasure 50/50 between
Windchaser and *Swiftwater,* be honest and fair with
each other, no bad temper—" she glanced at
Swiftwater's ship's boy — "and no sleeping on
watch!"

There was a deathly hush as everyone looked at Leo,
wondering what his reaction would be. Would he
really want to sign up with two ginger buccaneer
girls after they had taken the boat from under his nose
while he was sleeping and, although the words had
not been said, been accused of slacking?

Leo took a deep breath. What should he say? The
answer was obvious. Summer had even referred to it
in the code. Honesty.

He stood up and approached the girls, awkwardly

thrusting out his hand.

"I haven't started too well," he confessed, "and I apologise for that. Also, to the crew of *Swiftwater*. You are right. I did fall asleep on watch after being entrusted with our boat, and I was just making excuses. It won't happen again."

He shook hands with them all and sat down abruptly, red in the face from embarrassment.

Summer looked at Scarlett. "Well?" she asked.

"I'm sorry I took your boat," she responded. "Captain Summer said it was the wrong thing to do, but I couldn't resist. I honestly didn't mean to cause so much trouble."

Leo nodded. "You're okay," he responded. "And you handled her pretty well."

"Thank goodness for that," said Josh, "because here comes a police officer!"

A **rotund,** uniformed policeman was approaching the jetty.

"Please don't say it was me," pleaded Scarlett, "or I'll be in the most awful trouble."

"Leave it to me," said Josh, and he leapt to his feet and ran off towards the officer, with Jack following him.

There was agitated shouting from the police officer, who waved his arms, pointing back the way he had come. He shook his finger at Josh, who was standing with his head down and looking very **contrite**. They could hear Jack barking, and Josh grabbed him by the collar.

Then, the irate policeman marched off back the way he had come.

"Wow, was he angry or what?" exclaimed Josh. "He called me an idiot and said he'd had to walk all the way uphill to get here on a fool's errand! He even said Jack was savage just because he barked at him."

"He would," said Summer. "He's our uncle Shaun, and he's afraid of dogs and exercise!"

"So, that's why you didn't want him to know," said Josh.

"Thanks awfully," said Scarlett. "He'd have told Mum, and I would have been marooned at home for a month at least."

"What did you tell him?" asked Harper.

"I said I hadn't tied the boat properly, and it had drifted off."

"That must have been hard," said Scarlett, knowing how proud she was of her seamanship and how Josh would have felt about his. "Thank you, and I *really* am sorry I stole your boat."

"You didn't have to say it was you," said Leo. "It was my fault, after all."

Josh smiled. "It's okay, Leo. No harm done."

"Let's get on with the code," said Noz. "We've been here an awful long time, and I'm hungry!"

And so between them, the seven children drafted the joint Ship's Articles.

"Now, to sign," said Summer. "First Mate Scarlett."

"Aye, Captain," she responded and rummaged in the tin box, bringing out a pin and some cotton wool.

"Do any of you have any diseases?" queried Summer.

"Of course not!" said Freddie indignantly.

Summer laid out the paper in front of them. "I'll go first," she said, signing the bottom in pencil before pricking her thumb with the pin and pressing the bloody **digit** underneath.

She wiped her thumb and handed the pin and pencil to Freddie. "Now you. The pin has been disinfected, so it's okay."

Freddie grimaced but signed and added his fingerprint before handing it to Scarlett, who did the same.

Soon, all seven children had added their names and sealed the article in blood.

"Hold on," said Harper. "There's one more to add." She wrote 'Jack—Ship's Dog' on the paper before lifting Jack's paw and pressing it into the mud at the side of the jetty.

"Hereby signed and delivered," she said, imprinting Jack's muddy paw under his name.

Having done his duty, Jack wagged his tail and trotted off to explore a possible rabbit trail while the adventurers continued with the document.

"There's one last bit to read," said Summer, clearing her throat.

And so, young adventurers remember that even the wildest of sailors understood the importance of rules and order. Just like those fearless buccaneers of old, we too can learn the value of discipline, fairness, and unity in our own daring quests. As we navigate the uncharted waters of life, may the lessons of the buccaneers' code guide us towards a treasure trove of wisdom and adventure.

"She copied that from a book," whispered Scarlett, and Summer scowled at her before exclaiming,

"There's just one last thing to do to show our alliance and friendship."

She took off her red woollen hat and presented it to Harper. "I want you to have this," she said shyly, "if you don't mind a second-hand article?"

Harper was dumbfounded. "Are you sure? I mean, it seems almost a part of you. I don't know whether I can take such a gift."

"A gift that means nothing is not worth giving," replied Summer. "Please, I want you to have it to remind us of our new alliance. *Windchaser* and *Swiftwater,* forever!"

Harper took the hat, almost in awe, and put it on her head.

"No, not like that," laughed Summer, "you need to look a bit more swashbuckling!" She adjusted the hat so that it sat back on Harper's head, the way she wore it herself. "There, that's perfect, shipmate."

"I don't know what to say," said Harper. "Thank you doesn't seem anywhere near enough."

"We need to give you something," said Freddie, "but I don't think we have anything."

Josh interrupted. "Yes, we do," he said. "Scarlett, as first mate, I want you to have this. My dad gave it to me, and it's very special. As special as Summer's hat."

And he handed her his precious compass. "With it, you will never be lost, and you will always know the right way to go," he declared.

Chapter Fourteen

A Surprise

"So, having signed the Articles," concluded Freddie, "what next? What is the secret you want to share?"

"What is your intention about Shadowmere Island first?" asked Scarlett.

Freddie looked at his crew. "What do we tell them?"

"Everything," responded Josh. "Remember honesty? And I think we can trust the girls."

"Ship's Boy," directed Freddie, "fetch the map and the chart."

"Aye, aye, sir," responded Leo as he boarded *Swiftwater,* returning with the documents clutched in his hand.

Freddie spread them out on the jetty, weighing them down with stones.

"As you said, we are staying at Captain Jack's cottage. In one of the bedrooms is a painting of him, which was a clue that started us thinking."

"Yes," said Noz, "we had already decided that the island was a place to explore, and after speaking to an old fisherman on the beach, we decided to sail there and find the captain's last will and the treasure he'd hidden. The old man told us that someone had offered to buy the island, and the council or whoever had agreed. So time isn't on our side."

Summer looked at Harper. "This fisherman. Was he wearing big black waders?" she queried.

"He was!" she replied. "He could only just walk in them."

"Old fisherman!" snorted Scarlett. "It's Uncle Bob."

"Are you related to everyone here?" enquired Leo **incredulously.**

"Just about," replied Scarlett. "Our family has lived here for generations."

"Anyway," continued Freddie, "Noz here found a book with a verse that turned out to be a clue. Look." He handed the paper to Summer, and Scarlett read it over her shoulder.

Verily, amidst the grounded Rukhs, Fair Luna hath ceased her consumption at the tithe, but doth present Matthew a count of seven secure paths and a tally of thirteen treacherous ways.

"Whatever does that mean?" challenged Summer. "It's all in old English and makes no sense."

"That's what we thought at first," declared Harper, "but we worked it out between us."

"And with some help from our mum!" pointed out Josh.

"Here's what we came up with," said Freddie, handing Summer the translation.

Between the castles, when the moon is full at ten, take the narrow and safe way.

"I told you the castles on the island were important!" blurted out Scarlett to her sister.

"Okay, you were right," said Summer. "When is the full moon? Do we know?"

"Tonight," responded Josh.

"So, hadn't we better get out there?" said Scarlett urgently.

"We're okay until 2200 hours," responded Freddie. "But yes, we mustn't leave it too long."

"Do you know a safe passage into the cove?" enquired Summer.

Freddie smiled. "Of course." He handed her the chart that Harper had drawn.

"Cooperstown? Coopersland?" said Summer in a strained voice. "Why have you written that? There are no such places."

"I hope I haven't done anything wrong," began Harper, "but that was me. We know the original owner of the cottage—the man who disappeared—was named William Cooper. I thought the poor man needed to be remembered."

"There's also something you need to know," said Freddie, "that might just make you think twice about joining us."

Summer and Scarlett exchanged worried looks.

"Okay," responded Summer slowly, "what is that?"

Freddie recounted the weasel-faced man who had tried to steal the captain's book and had taken the original old map of the island.

"We know him," responded Scarlett furiously. "He's a local thief and an all-round bad guy named Jamie Jenkins who'll do anything for money. We'll have to be careful; he can be violent and has been snooping around Shadowmere Island. Recently, he caught us there, threatened us and told us not to go back."

"He tried it with us, but Freddie—" began Leo.

Freddie stopped him mid-flow. "Don't worry," he responded, "we'll watch ourselves."

"I don't suppose he's related to you?" queried Noz.

Summer and Scarlett smiled. "Thankfully, no," answered Summer. "But we have watched him, and he's up to no good. He's also been sneaking around the cottage you're staying at and meeting with some tweedy stranger in town."

"She means Cooperstown," Scarlett said, and Harper smiled.

"Thank you for Coopersland and Cooperstown. William would have loved that!" said Summer.

"William?" queried Harper.

"William Cooper," explained Scarlett.

"So, having done all this work, what are you hoping for?" asked Summer.

"To find Captain Jack's will and lost treasure!" exclaimed Leo excitedly.

"That's awkward," said Scarlett.

"Because our name is Cooper," confided Summer.

"Oh my," exclaimed Harper. "Poor William Cooper was your ancestor?"

"It was a long time ago," answered Scarlett, "but our family has always been accused of being thieves and related to pirates. But William wasn't a pirate. He was a trader who made his money honestly. Jack Swiftwater stole everything he had and left all the following generations of Coopers **impoverished**. And he probably did away with William, too."

"I am sorry," consoled Harper, "but perhaps we can put things right now that we have the map and the chart?"

Summer exchanged their secret twins look with Scarlett before nodding in agreement at the unspoken question.

"There is one more thing," said Summer. "The island

belongs to the Cooper family. We know because of letters and other documents from the past."

Freddie and the others were astonished.

"You mean you own an island all to yourself?" responded Josh.

"We do, but the trouble is, we can't prove it," said Scarlett. "Our family tried, but the authorities wouldn't accept the papers they had. They said they weren't legal documents because the signatures weren't witnessed properly."

"When our ancestor William Cooper went missing, that rogue Captain Jack somehow got the deeds to the island and the cottage and just moved in," continued Summer.

"And there was no will?" responded Freddie.

"It was never found," said Scarlett. "But if we can find Jack Swiftwater's will or some other legal papers, that might be sufficient for the authorities to reconsider."

"So," said Summer sadly, "that makes things difficult between *Windchaser* and *Swiftwater.* You're hoping to find treasure, and you've done so much work. We would never have been able to decipher the clues or even find the chart and map."

"I don't see the problem," responded Harper.

"Don't you see," said Summer, "if we are successful, then any treasure would have to be restored to the Cooper family? Even the island, if we find any legal evidence. And it's the adults who would deal with that. I don't think they'd take much notice of what we say."

"There isn't a problem. If it belongs to you, then it's

only right you have it," responded Harper. "We wouldn't dream of trying to keep any of it."

"*Swiftwater,*" said Freddie, "are all in agreement?"

He wasn't disappointed. The reply was unanimous. "Aye, Captain!"

Summer and Scarlett looked at each other, unable to believe what they had heard. They had never had such friends before. To give up any hope of keeping treasure, and perhaps an island too, was something too breathtaking for them to understand.

"I knew you were the right person to wear my hat," exclaimed Scarlett to Harper, picking up the chart to disguise the tears in her eyes. She studied it for a moment. "So, that's the way in. We've been trying to find it for years!"

"You haven't been to the island then?" asked Leo curiously.

"Oh, yes. Many times," confirmed Summer, "but we've had to anchor *Windchaser* offshore and swim in."

"That's risky, isn't it?" observed Leo, mindful of his limited swimming ability.

"We're both strong swimmers, and we know the current," affirmed Summer, "but it is inconvenient, as we haven't been able to go there at night or stay for any length of time."

"Probably just as well. Our parents would freak out at the very thought! And as we said, Jamie Jenkins chased us off the island once, so it could be dangerous," said Scarlett.

"Does he know the safe passage to the cove?" asked Noz. "How did he get there?"

"We don't know that," replied Scarlett. "We've never

seen a boat."

"Then let's waste no more time," said Freddie. "It's high time we explored Shadowmere Island and put a stop to the untruths about William Cooper and restore everything to its rightful owner."

"Hurrah for that!" shouted Summer and Scarlett.

And little Jack barked as if in agreement. When his beloved children were happy, he was happy too. And now he had two new friends in Summer and Scarlett Cooper, heiresses to the lost fortune of William Cooper, stolen by Captain Jack Swiftwater!

Chapter Fifteen

A Light to Your Path

"Would your parents let you stay on the island for the night?" asked Josh.

"No chance," retorted Scarlett. "They see everything as a risk. They are health and safety crazy!"

"That's a bit unfair," responded Summer. "They just worry about us, that's all."

"That's a pity," said Freddie. "Tonight is the last full moon for some time, and we have to return home to school at the end of the week. So, it's now or never."

"I think we may have a way," added Scarlett, "if Captain Summer agrees because it involves night sailing."

"I know exactly what you're thinking," guessed Summer. "We did it last year and got into a whole lot of trouble!"

Scarlett looked to the *Swiftwater* crew for support. "We can sneak out after dark," she said, "and if you can somehow light the safe channel to the island, we can join you later."

Freddie deferred to Scarlett's twin. "Summer's your captain; I can't interfere with her decision."

"Come on," implored Scarlett to her sister. "The Coopers have suffered from insults about being criminals and pirates over the centuries. Are we going to give up the only chance to find out what happened to William and restore the family honour

115

because of a little health and safety concern?"

Summer was silent for a while, thinking. Then she said, "Okay, but only because we have the *Swiftwater* crew to assist."

"Brilliant!" exclaimed Scarlett, performing a little jig on the jetty.

"We need some form of lighting," declared Josh. "Do you girls have anything? It must be bright enough to show up clearly in the dark."

"We have some old hurricane lamps. How many do you need?" enquired Summer.

Josh turned to his brother, putting the chart in front of him. "What do you think, Freddie? I reckon on at least three." He indicated on the chart. "One on the castle to the north of that triangular rock, one on the triangular marker itself, and one on the port side of the safe channel to mark the underwater rocks."

"I agree," responded Freddie. "Captain Summer?"

"That will be fine," she said. "I can get three paraffin lamps. They will do the trick."

"Right," replied Freddie, checking his watch. "We'd better get a move on. We'll make a circuit of the island to check it out if you can rendezvous with us just off Shadowmere in an hour to give us the lamps." He marked the chart with a cross. "This is the **RV** point. Then we'll moor in the cove and ensure it's safe. You must be back by **twenty-thirty hours** at the latest. It will be dark then, and we'll set the lamps. We don't want to light them too early in case Jamie Jenkins and his mate see them."

"Aye, aye, Captain Freddie," responded Summer as she boarded *Windchaser,* followed by the first mate. She put the tiller hard to port, and Scarlett heaved on

116

the halyard. As it rose, the mainsail filled, and they headed away from the jetty and across the water. "Come on, *Swiftwater* crew, there's no time to waste," ordered Captain Freddie, and soon, their boat was underway, heading out from Cooperstown in the wake of *Windchaser.*

"We should sing a Sea Shanty," encouraged Josh. "Freddie and I know one from sailing with Dad. Do you remember it, Freddie?"

"Of course!" he responded. "I think we'll change a couple of words, though."

And he and Josh launched into the song:

Farewell and adieu, to you Spanish ladies
Farewell and adieu, to you ladies of Spain
For we received orders
For to sail for old Shadowmere,
But we hope, very soon, we shall see you again

We'll rant and we'll roar like true British sailors
We'll rant and we'll roar along the salt seas
Until we strike soundings in the channel of Old
England
From Coopersland to Shadowmere is only four
leagues.

The crew of *Swiftwater* and *Windchaser* joined in, their happy voices travelling across the expanse of water between the two vessels. It was a fitting tribute for a voyage to a treasure island.

They parted with a final wave, the Coopers making their way toward home along the coast to the southeast to collect the hurricane lamps. At the same time, Freddie and his crew took their bearing northeast to **circumnavigate** Shadowmere Island.

The brisk wind propelled them on, the flag at their masthead fluttering vibrantly as they embarked on their grand expedition. Adventure beckoned. To explore the mysteries of Shadowmere and prepare for the after-dark landing of Captain Summer and First Mate Scarlett. To begin the quest for the long-lost secrets of Jack Swiftwater and the restoration of all that the pirate captain had stolen from William Cooper.

Chapter Sixteen

Safe Haven

They navigated around the island in under an hour but found no suitable place to land other than that shown on their chart.

As they had observed earlier, most of the island was surrounded by rugged rocks, a natural fortress against invaders.

"It's time to RV with *Windchaser*," announced Freddie. "Ship's Boy!"

"Aye, Captain?" responded Leo.

"Sing out when you sight them."

Leo scanned across the water through the binoculars and shortly afterwards, shouted out as the white sail of their allies came into view.

"Sail ho! On the starboard bow."

"Ready about," called Freddie. "Gybo!"

He put the tiller down, and *Swiftwater* responded, the crew ducking as the sail swept across and she settled onto her new course.

Scarlett was just as vigilant, and she soon spied them and waved enthusiastically.

Windchaser came alongside, Scarlett dropped the mainsail, and Josh lowered *Swiftwater's*. Then he took hold of their gunwale to hold their boat steady.

Scarlett handed over the three hurricane lamps and a small can of paraffin.

"The lamps are full," she explained, "and there's

some extra oil here in case you need it. And matches, of course."

"Come on, Scarlett," said Summer urgently. "We must get back home before we're missed."

Josh released the boat, and Scarlett pulled on the halyard. The sail rose, and *Windchaser* headed away.

"Twenty-thirty hours!" Freddie called after them. "We'll be keeping a weather eye out for you."

Summer waved; the boat heeled over as she put the helm hard to port, and soon it was just a speck in the distance.

"Ship's Boy!" called out Captain Freddie to Leo, positioned at the boat's **fore**.

"Aye, aye," he responded.

"We're going to be navigating into the bay. Keep alert for hidden rocks and shallows as we go. You're in the best place to spot anything."

Josh raised the sail and Freddie set a course for Shadowmere Island, keeping close to land to avoid the hidden dangers marked on the chart. At first, the going was easy as they were **running before the wind**, but after passing to the southeast of Coopersland, the wind's direction changed, blowing in directly from the east.

"We need to tack," said Freddie. "We can't make way with the wind blowing straight at us."

He put the tiller to starboard.

"Ready about. Gybo!"

Swiftwater responded by turning to port, the boom passing safely over the heads of the crew as it changed course.

Freddie made a series of short tacks back and forth, each time moving further east and gradually nearer to Shadowmere Island.

"Rocks on the starboard bow," sang out Harper, and Freddie reacted by putting the helm down, and the boat gallantly responded on its new bearing.

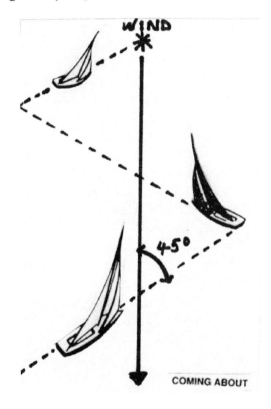

COMING ABOUT

"We need the chart, Harper," said Freddie, "to navigate our route into Smugglers' Cove."

She placed it on the centre thwart so that Freddie and Josh could see it, weighing it down with the **rowlocks** secured to **lanyards**.

"We need to head due north," said Josh, "towards that

121

castle."

Freddie lifted the binoculars to his eyes.

"Yes, toward the castle we go," he responded, "and I can see now what that triangle marked on the chart is."

He handed the glasses to Josh. "Look."

"It's a triangular rock," he replied. "Or almost a triangle. It looks like a chunk of it has fallen into the *Mere*."

"Let me have a look, please," said Harper.

She adjusted the glasses and studied the island intently.

"It was probably a triangular **edifice** at some stage," she observed, "but I'm not surprised that some of it has crumbled after a couple of centuries."

"So, Captain," said Josh, "you need to line up the tip of that rock carefully with the castle, which is the safe channel into the cove."

"We have to make sure to keep to starboard as we enter," responded Freddie. "And slow as we get near. We'll lose the wind anyway as we get close to the tall rocks and into the shelter of the channel, but *Swiftwater* will have enough way on her to take us safely into our mooring. We have the oars to help us if we need them."

They entered the **lee** of the passage, and Freddie called out, "Lower the sail!"

"Aye, aye," responded Josh, and as it dropped, he grabbed handfuls of it, wrapping it around the boom and tying it off out of the way.

"Leo!" called out Freddie, "keep your eyes sharp now; we're coming into an area where there are a lot of submerged rocks. If we hit one, we'll be in big trouble and likely sink."

"Phew," responded First Mate Josh, "thanks a lot for the encouragement, skipper."

Freddie lined up the distant castle on the hill with the once triangular-shaped rock before him, edging *Swiftwater* steadily forward and scanning the area for dangers.

"Rocks on the port bow!" called out the ship's boy. Captain Freddie responded by steering closer to the rock wall on the starboard side.

"Noz," he said, "go forward to the bow with Leo and take an oar with you. If we get too close to any rocks, you can use it to fend us off."

He turned to Josh. "We're losing **momentum**," he said, "now that we've lost the wind in the lee of these rock walls. I'm going to **scull** to keep us moving. I haven't done this for a long time, but we don't want to drift onto any rocks."

Freddie lowered his oar over the stern of the boat and waggled it back and forth in figure of eight movements, propelling them gradually forward.

With Leo and Noz in the bow, rock spotting, they manoeuvred through the channel until their boat slid with ease onto the sandy beach in the cove. The crew jumped ashore, pulling *Swiftwater* up and onto the beach.

"We've made it!" cried out Noz. "Safe haven and Shadowmere Island at last!"

Chapter Seventeen

The Cave

The Six stood on the beach, the children staring in awe at the cliffs above them.

Now that they were seeing the island close-up, it was even more **formidable** than it had first appeared. The cliffs flanking them on both sides seemed to stretch up endlessly, like giant protectors of a secret haven, the sheer rock faces appearing to reach for the heavens.

Boulders dotted the sandy beach as if they had been scattered there by some ancient giant's hand, their surfaces weathered by years of wind and water, the rough textures a testament to the power of the elements.

Trees reached upwards, their branches a tangle of leaves. Perhaps they murmured secrets to each other as they rustled in the wind, creating a symphony that only children could hear.

At the base of the cliffs, mysterious caves beckoned. Dark openings in the rock formations that hinted at hidden passages. What secrets might they hold?

Caught up in the excitement, Jack frolicked along the shoreline, chasing seagulls and leaving pawprints in the sand. His joyful barks echoed against the soaring cliffs, a reminder that even in the awe-inspiring landscape, the simple pleasure of a dog at play had its own magic.

Shadows grew longer, casting a glow across the cove, and the children somehow knew that this moment, this memory, was something extraordinary in their young lives, etched into the very fabric of time. A place where dreams of adventure and reality intertwined, and the island whispered secrets that only the heart of a child could understand.

Noz was the one who ended the spell.

"I'm hungry," he said.

The others then realised they, too, had not eaten since breakfast.

"We must get set up before dark," said Freddie. "We need to unload the boat, make our camp, eat and put the hurricane lamps in place."

Harper surveyed the area and pointed to a rough track leading upwards from the cove.

"We should move from here," she advised. "The *Mere* is tidal, and you'll remember how we were almost trapped by the tide on the beach in Cornwall last summer! I'll check it out for a suitable place to make camp."

As Harper nimbly went upwards, with Jack running ahead, the others tied *Swiftwater* to a boulder before unloading it and stacking everything high on the beach.

"There's no need to take the lamps," said Freddie. "Look, we can store them in that cave over there."

Noz picked them up and carried them to the opening in the rocks, disappearing inside.

"You've forgotten the extra paraffin!" shouted Leo, but Noz was out of earshot by then.

"I'll take it," he said, following Noz's sand footprints into the cave.

Time passed, and Jack and Harper returned to the beach.

"I've found the perfect spot," she said. "It's dry, flat and grassy, out of the wind and far enough from any trees that might decide to drop branches on us."

"Well done," replied Josh. "Let's get all this stuff up there and sort something to eat. Noz! Leo!"

He stood up. "They only went in to store the lamps. They've been gone an awful long time."

Feeling concerned, they hurried over to the mouth of the cave, and Jack raced in ahead of them.

"Noz! Leo!" called Freddie. But there was no answer.

"It's dark inside," observed Harper. "Here, take my torch."

Freddie switched it on. The beam lit up the interior, and the cave came to life as the dancing light cast shifting shadows across the rugged walls, revealing a **labyrinthine** network of crevices and formations. The air was cool and slightly damp, carrying an earthy aroma that mingled with the faint scent of aged and weathered rock, their surfaces textured and uneven, adorned with mineral deposits glistening in the torchlight. Occasional patches of moss and lichen clung to the rock, adding a touch of muted colour to the otherwise grey scene. Stalactites hung from the ceiling like jagged teeth, occasionally catching the light so that they appeared to come alive, their shapes appearing to shift and morph as if they possessed a life of their own.

A tunnel in front of them narrowed as it wound its way around a bend before disappearing from immediate sight. The sound of dripping water echoed ahead from some unseen source.

"Noz! Leo! Where are you?" shouted Freddie.

But there came no answer.

Meanwhile, Jack was having a fine time sniffing around with fresh smells to enjoy.

One smell, however, wasn't at all pleasant. There are certain scents from people that, to a dog, speak of bad character. And Jack smelled one at that very moment.

It was the unpleasant odour of a **villain**!

Chapter Eighteen

Ransom

"*Où sont-ils allés*—where have they got to?" questioned Josh worriedly. "They were only meant to store the lamps somewhere safe, not go exploring."

"And it won't be all that long before it's dark, and we've got to get those lamps in place for *Windchaser*," said Freddie, "or they won't be able to navigate into the channel."

"We've also got to be in position on top of the island before the full moon at ten," added Josh.

"We must look for the boys first," responded Harper, "in case something has happened to them. Let me have my torch."

She set off determinedly down the tunnel, with Freddie and Josh following.

Jack ran on and soon vanished, blending invisibly into the darkness ahead.

The three children increased their speed and came to a crossroads, with a tunnel going off in each direction.

"Which way?" said Harper.

The question was answered for them as they heard Jack barking in the distance.

"Come on," urged Freddie, taking the left fork, "If Jack's gone this way, that's where Noz and Leo will be!"

"Look," said Harper, pointing to the ground,

"something is very wrong!"

There lay the three hurricane lamps Noz had taken into the cave. There was a heady odour and a wet patch on the rock floor where the paraffin had leaked. Harper promptly set them upright. "I don't know how much fuel is left in them," she said, "but the boys are more important now. And Jack is still barking. I don't like the sound of that."

They continued down the tunnel, Jack's barking growing louder as they went until they rounded a bend and saw the cause.

Their dog was tied to a metal bar set in the wall. He was growling and barking at the man standing just out of his reach.

"It's weasel face Jenkins!" exclaimed Freddie, running forward.

"You stay where you are, you blighter," said the man to Freddie in a coarse voice, raising the iron bar he was holding threateningly. "Unless you want the dog to get some of this!" He recognised Freddie as the boy who had thrown him to the ground at Swiftwater Cottage, and he didn't want to tangle with him again.

Freddie stopped in his tracks, glaring. "If you hurt my dog, you'll be very sorry," he vowed.

"There's no need for that," said the man, with an evil-looking grin, "if you do what you're told."

"What do you want, you awful man?" shouted Harper fearlessly. "And where are our friends?"

The man laughed. "Awful man? You'd better believe that, miss. Now, get in there. You'll find your friends waiting for you."

He pointed to a wooden door set in the wall. "Don't you worry your little head," he said to Harper

condescendingly. "It's just an old smugglers' store cupboard with no creepy crawlies."

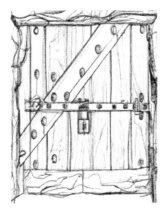

Jack had stopped barking now that the children had arrived, but he continued to growl.

"Go on, in you go," repeated the man.

"What about our dog?" said Josh.

"When you do what you're told and give me what I want," he said, "you'll have him back. Call it a **ransom**."

The children reluctantly filed through the door, leaving Jack outside, and were greeted by Noz and Leo inside.

The door slammed shut behind them, and they were in darkness.

"Thank goodness you are both okay," said Harper, switching her torch back on. "We were so worried about you."

"What happened?" asked Freddie.

"We were caught by surprise," responded Noz. "Old weasel face was hiding in the cave; He has this iron

131

bar, and when Jack came running up, he threatened to hurt him unless we tied him up. Then he shut us in this storeroom."

"Did you notice he was dripping wet?" asked Harper.

"It was hard to miss," replied Leo. "I suppose he fell in the water."

"Good," said Harper. "He deserves it!"

"What do you want?" shouted Freddie through the door, although he had some idea, after having caught the man trying to steal Captain Jack's book.

"The treasure map is all I want," was the reply, "and the clue to where it's hidden. It's in that little book you took from me! Hand them over, and you can all go free."

"It wasn't your book in the first place," stated Freddie defiantly. "You have no right to it."

"Right or wrong, that's the deal," was the answer.

"And you don't touch little Jack," demanded Harper, "or there is no deal."

There was a moment's silence before the response came.

"Ok, but you don't get him until I'm safe out of the way."

"Do you have the map?" said Freddie to Harper.

She reached into her pocket. "It's here. Do we have to give it to him?"

"It's that or Jack might get hurt. Jamie Jenkins seems nasty enough to do it."

"What about the clue?"

"Do you have both versions of it?" asked Freddie.

Harper handed them over.

"Shine your torch over here," said Freddie. "And let me have your pen, please." He ripped a blank strip from the paper containing the cryptic clue and hastily re-wrote the translation, keeping the original, which he stuffed in his trouser pocket.

"Do you want to come and get them?" shouted Freddie.

"Nice try," responded Jenkins, "but no. You were lucky the last time we met and caught me off guard. *That* won't happen again. Just slide them through the gap under the door."

"How do we know you'll keep your side of the bargain?" said Josh.

"You have little choice," was the gruff reply. "And I'll be checking them, so don't try any funny stuff."

Freddie folded them and slid them through the gap. He could hear the faint crackle of the paper as the man picked them up and opened them.

Then there was silence.

"Are you there?" shouted Josh.

There was still no reply.

"He's just gone off and left us," responded Leo angrily.

"I'm not surprised," muttered Noz. "You can't trust a man like that."

"So," said Harper. "What do we do now?"

Chapter Nineteen

Castles Carved by Giants

"I haven't done this before," said Noz, "but there's a chance with an old door like this…" He felt the hinges at the side.

"Can you light this up, Harper?" he asked.

Harper shone the fading beam of her torch, and Noz gave a small cheer of self-congratulation.

"As I'd hoped. Give me a hand, Freddie and Josh. We can lift the door off its hinges if it's not too rusted or heavy!"

Freddie and Josh joined Noz in gripping the door as best they could, although there weren't any good handholds.

"Right, lift!" grunted Noz.

The boys strained as hard as they could, and the door moved slightly.

"It's heavy," panted Noz. "I'm not sure we can do it."

The torchlight shifted, and for a moment, the boys were left in shadow as Harper moved to the back of the store. "There are some rusty old tools on a shelf," she said. "An old saw and a hammer. I don't know if they'll be much help, but…"

There was a smashing sound, and she returned, directing the torch beam back onto the door. "But this might. Let's try it."

She was holding a length of oak wood that had once been the shelf. "If I slide it under the door, I can use

135

it as a lever if you boys lift at the same time."

She pushed it into the gap at the base of the door until it was halfway through. "Okay," she called, "lift!" Harper heaved on the wooden lever, and the boys put all their strength into lifting the door. It resisted for a moment, then rose off its hinges. It collapsed outwards into the tunnel with a resounding crash, the weight ripping the lock apart as it fell, a heavy cloud of dust rising into the air.

"Good thinking, Harper," said Freddie. "Come on; we must get out of here." He apprehensively peered down the smoggy tunnel. "Jack!" he called.

A bark came from behind the fog of dust, and Freddie ran through it to find his beloved dog.

"He's okay, although dirty," he shouted, appearing through the cloud with Jack in his arms.

Despite the urgency, the children could not resist a few moments of fussing with the dog, who promptly rolled onto his back, peddled his paws in the air, and getting even dirtier.

"Thank goodness he's okay," cried Harper. "If that man had hurt him…"

"He's all right, Harper," said Leo comfortingly. "And we'll make sure the weasel doesn't get his hands on him again."

The Secret Six hurried down the tunnel and out onto the beach. Jack, none the worse for his time of captivity, ran ahead and leapt into the sea, swimming happily in a circle until Freddie called him back.

"Well, at least he's clean now," laughed Harper.

Although starting to go down, the sunlight was still blinding after the cave's darkness, and they screwed up their eyes until they adjusted to the light.

"I think that's him!" called out Josh, pointing across the water, before running over to their pile of equipment still stacked on the beach. He grabbed the binoculars and scanned the *Mere*.

"It's Jenkins all right. He's in a motorboat and heading toward Cooperstown."

"He must have got here the same way as Summer and Scarlett. Moored away from the island and swam into the cove," responded Josh. "That's why he was wet."

"Then he'll try to bring the boat into the cove, now he knows the safe route," Freddie said gravely. "I would guess he's going to pick up that tweedy man."

"And he knows the clues to the treasure," said Leo.

"Not quite," responded Freddie with a smile.

"How so?" said Harper.

"I slightly re-wrote part of the clue before letting Jenkins have it," replied Freddie.

"What did you do?" asked Josh, a big grin lighting up his face.

Freddie recited the clue he'd re-written from memory.

Between the castles, when the moon is full, take the wide and safe way.

He emphasised the word 'wide.' "Just a tiny alteration," said Freddie, "but enough that they'll never find the treasure. If they take the wide path instead of the narrow way, they could wander around in a maze of caves for hours and hours!"

Noz laughed. "He and his mate deserve that," he said. "He's no better than a pirate and was going to leave us shut up in the cave."

"Pirates? That's just what they are! But perhaps we still have some chance to claim Summer and Scarlett's inheritance?" said Harper optimistically.

"We do, but we need to make plans and be ready," Josh asserted, "before they return. I wonder who that tweedy man is that Summer spoke of?"

"Perhaps he's the one who wants to buy the island?" said Leo.

"If he is, we need to find Captain Jack's will and any treasure before he does. We can't let Summer and Scarlett down," said Harper anxiously.

The children burst into a whirlwind of activity, carrying their camping equipment and food to the place at the top of the island that Harper had found. "I can't see us sleeping much tonight," said Noz, although they set up their tents and sleeping bags just in case.

Harper pulled the cover off the wicker basket the twins' mum had provided and put the food on paper plates, using a convenient flat rock as a table.

"Your mum," she told the twins, "knows how to look after us. She's put so much in that even Noz can't eat the lot!"

Noz pretended to be deeply hurt and gave them an injured look.

But that didn't stop him from tucking in, and once they had all eaten, Freddie said, "We need to get down to the serious business of deciding what we're going to do. The pirates will be back, and we've got to be ready for them. Suggestions?"

"We have to prevent them from landing; it's as simple as that," asserted Josh.

"Okay," responded Freddie. "Next?"

"We must have some kind of backup plan in case they abandon their boat and swim to shore," suggested Harper. "That's how Jenkins got here."

"I'll give that some thought," said Josh.

"Great," said Freddie. "Share it with us when you've worked out the details. Anything else?"

"We have to be in the right place at the top of the island for when the full moon reveals the treasure's location," said Harper. "If we don't, all this will be a waste of time. And the Coopers will be swindled out of their inheritance again!"

"You're right, Harper," said Josh. "But don't worry. Let's scout Shadowmere and find the best spot to view both castles for when the moon rises."

"I'll go with Harper, and no doubt Jack will follow," said Freddie, "and you, Josh, go with Leo. Noz, would you keep watch in case the pirates come back early? There's a decent view across the water from here. They might not wait until after dark, but probably won't take any chances."

Noz was more than happy not to have to climb any steep inclines. "I'll look after the food," he exclaimed.

"You leave it alone," cautioned Harper. "I'll be checking it when I get back, and if you've been scoffing it…" She left the sentence unfinished, but Noz had an idea of what she meant.

"You two head for the southern castle," suggested Freddie, "and Harper and I will investigate the northern one. Then meet back here, and we'll check out the terrain below together."

Josh and Leo set off. It was tough going, but they

finally reached the ruined castle standing at a high point of the island.

Despite its ruin, the weathered sentinel stood, its walls crumbled and scarred by time and the elements, yet still magnificent. It nestled upon a craggy clifftop, a place of mystery where time seemed to have stood still, but the echoes of the ancient past danced upon the winds.

How would this have been in Captain Jack's day, wondered Leo, when most uneducated folk strongly believed in superstition? In popular folk law, dragons roamed, and wizards wielded their powers, and perhaps this castle was built as a stronghold to protect the land from dark forces that sought to conquer it. Perhaps mighty giants constructed it, shaping stone as if it were clay, and the castle's towers reached the sky, holding secrets and treasures beyond imagination.

Josh and Leo stood beside it, gazing across the shimmering expanse of water, feeling like they were at the world's edge. A mesmerising picture conjured up in their imagination of ships and sea creatures that once navigated these very waters as the seagulls wheeled overhead, their cries echoing across the landscape and lending an eerie atmosphere to their surroundings.

From ages long past, what men had stood in that very place, staring out, where the sun rose like a blazing golden gem in the morning sky to cast its warm embrace upon the land? And when night finally fell, did the stars above twinkle like ancient diamonds, revealing their stories to those who dared to dream?

"Come on," said Josh, "let's see what the inside is

like."

Tall grasses and wildflowers brushed against their legs as they made their way through the overgrown path leading toward the interior of the castle. As they ventured deeper inside, excitement and nervousness gripped them. Sunlight streaming through gaps in the brickwork cast dappled patterns on the decaying floor. Their footsteps echoed in the silence, and the air inside was musty and damp.

They saw the *Mere* stretching out to the horizon and Coopersland beyond through a gap in the crumbling wall. And a strange feeling of being disconnected from the world outside the island filled them with a sense of vulnerability.

The boys exchanged nervous glances, feeling a twinge of unease.

"Let's go," said Leo. "I think we've seen enough, don't you?"

"I agree," responded Josh. "There's something strange about this place, which gives me the creeps."

Chapter Twenty

Preparing the Defences

The four met again on the island's high point, surveying the rock-strewn valley below them.

"That castle is the strangest place," reported Josh. "There is a weird feeling about it—almost as if it lives in the past. I know that makes little sense," he continued, "but I don't know how else to describe it. It gave me the jitters."

"It freaked me out," declared Leo.

"I know what you mean," responded Harper. "Freddie and I said that our castle had a strange air about it. And Jack didn't want to go inside."

"Really, odd," said Freddie. "But let's check out below so we know what we're dealing with when it gets dark. This is your area, Josh. Do you want to take the lead?"

Josh nodded his agreement and descended the path leading to the **gorge** between the two castles.

The valley's centre had many caves and winding tracks, each presenting different challenges. There were caverns of all sizes, some broad and inviting, while others were narrow and mysterious, daring the Secret Six to venture within. But which track should they take? The wide paths beckoned to them, a comfortable route well-trodden by explorers of the distant past.

Besides these, the narrow passages looked far more

challenging. They twisted and turned with tight squeezes and dimly lit chambers. Those journeys looked far more complex and dangerous.

"I wonder what the full moon will reveal," said Harper. "If not for the warning, I would have chosen one of the easier routes where the path is wide and the journey smooth. The narrow paths seem to be more treacherous. And they all seem to head in the same direction anyway, so why not make it easy?"

Freddie checked his watch. "As tempting as it is, we haven't got the time to check out any of these now. We must get back to Noz. The afternoon is moving on, and we've got to set the hurricane lamps up for *Windchaser and* prepare a welcome for the pirates."

"They'll be making some kind of move soon," said Harper.

"So we don't have much time," replied Josh. "We have to get our plan sorted and then get on with it!"

They returned to camp, where Noz was waiting contentedly for them.

Harper eyed him with suspicion. "Have you been at the food?" she demanded.

Noz was a picture of innocence. "You are so mistrustful," he replied.

"That's not an answer," said Harper.

Noz admitted, "Maybe just a small piece of cake, but being on guard duty is exhausting."

Freddie just laughed. "Okay, we'll let you off. Any sign of pirate boats heading our way?"

"Not so much as a glimpse, Captain," he replied.

"So, let's get down to the cove," directed Freddie.

They descended the path, and Jack met them at the bottom.

"We have to think about how to keep the channel open for *Windchaser* but prevent Jamie Jenkins and his mate from bringing their boat in," mused Freddie.

"We don't know when they will come," responded Leo.

Harper said, "One of us should go to the high point of the island with binoculars and keep watch, then signal if they see anything."

"That triangular landmark is as good a place as any and easy to climb. I suggest Leo for that job," said Freddie.

"And how do I signal?" asked Leo.

"It's bound to be after dark, so you can use the hurricane lamp. You can wave it back and forth to warn us."

"What about if it's *Windchaser?*" said Leo. "We need two signals. One for the pirates and the other for the Coopers."

"Good thought," said Josh. "If it's a friendly boat, wave the lamp up and down. If it's the scurvy pirates, wave it from side to side. Got that?"

"Of course," said Leo. "Up and down Cooperstown. Left to right, pirates in sight!"

"That's clever, Leo," said Harper in admiration.

"I've been thinking," said Josh. "We can use a fallen tree or driftwood to create a makeshift barricade across the channel. That will stop the pirate's boat from entering the cove and even damage it if they attempt to force their way through."

"That's an idea," said Freddie.

Harper took out her pencil. "Paper, anyone?" she said.

"Here." Freddie handed her the slip he'd torn from the chart.

She sketched the route into the cove. "The channel is about five metres wide at its narrowest point, so that's where we need to put our **blockade**," she said. Then she drew a tree positioned against the rock wall of the channel, with a rope tied to its upper trunk. "When we pull the rope, the tree will pivot across the channel and block it," she explained. "We just have to hope the Cooper girls get in here with *Windchaser* before the pirates arrive. Otherwise, they'll get shut out."

"That's brilliant," said Leo, "but where do we get a rope and a tree from?"

Josh pointed at *Swiftwater.* "Some of what we need is right there," he responded.

"We use our boat?" Leo asked incredulously.

"Just the halyard and perhaps another rope," replied Josh.

Harper pointed to a high point above the rock face. "And as for the tree, take your pick," she responded. "There's bound to be one or two fallen ones up there."

They looked up at the cluster of trees growing along the edge of the cliffs above the cove.

"If there's one near the cliff edge, perhaps we can just roll it over," replied Noz. "But we might have to cut some branches off first."

"What about that old saw I found in the store?" exclaimed Harper. "I don't know how strong it will be after rusting away all these years."

"We can try it," responded Josh. "I'll get it if the rest of you want to follow Noz."

146

Josh ran back to the cave with Jack trotting ahead of him while the others ascended the steep path back to the top of the island.

"I need a rest," Noz puffed. "It's a beast of a climb!" They waited at the top, until Josh came running up to them, waving the rusty saw above his head. "Have you found a tree?"

Freddie patted the one lying on the ground next to him.

Jack sniffed it attentively. There were obviously interesting smells there. It was positioned perfectly beside the cliff edge and immediately above the passage to the cove.

"If we roll it, it'll fall straight over the edge," said Harper. "And you were right, Noz. Some branches need to be removed first."

"That looks like a two-man logging saw, Josh," said Noz, examining it with interest. "What luck!"

He hastily handed it back. "You and Freddie are better at all this physical stuff than I am!"

Freddie smiled. "Come on, Josh."

He took one end of the saw's handle, and his twin brother grabbed the other, and together, they started cutting at the branches.

Both boys worked hard. It didn't take long, and they soon stripped the tree.

"Leo, make sure Jack stays safe and away from here," Harper told her brother. "He's a bit too interested in what we're doing."

Leo attached a leash to Jack's collar and moved him to a safe distance.

Then, they rolled the log towards the cliff edge.

"Get ready, guys. Mind your fingers! On the count of three," Josh shouted. "*Un, deux, trois, Tomber—Timber!*"

With a last heave, it went over the edge, reluctantly surrendering the patch of ground it had occupied for so many years. At first, it descended almost in slow motion before picking up speed and plunging into the cove far below with a great splash.

Chapter Twenty-One

Blockade

"You left them locked in a cave?" said Black Bart Worthington angrily.

The two men were standing on the public jetty at Cooperstown, looking across the M*ere* to the distant island of Shadowmere.

Jamie Jenkins shrugged his shoulders and mumbled a reply. "I didn't know what else to do. One boy is a real hooligan, and their dog is a fierce savage. If I had released them, they would have attacked me and taken the map."

"You're a fool," was the response. "Stealing a map is one thing, but shutting up kids in a cave is something entirely different. I don't care about *them*, but I do care about being imprisoned for a very long time."

"What do you want me to do?" he whined.

Black Bart sighed, thrusting his hands into the pockets of his tweed jacket. "When we land on the island, I'll sort it out myself, since you seem unable to think. I'm wondering what I'm paying you for."

"Without me, you'll never find the treasure, even if you have bought the island," retorted Jenkins. "You'll spend the rest of your life digging holes and searching for it!"

Black Bart didn't reply, but walked down the jetty to where the powerboat was moored.

"We'll leave after dark. We don't want any fishermen

to see us. By following your map to the treasure, I'll find out if I've wasted my money or not. Then we'll deal with the kids."

"Deal with them?" said Jenkins. "Surely you don't mean..?"

✳✳✳

The five children stood staring at the toppled tree, half lying on the sand and the rest in the water.

"Are we going to be able to move it?" asked Harper uncertainly. "It looks pretty cumbersome."

"Absolutely," responded Noz confidently. "Once it's in the water, it will float and be easy to manoeuvre into place. Lumberjacks do it all the time."

"Just so you know," said Harper, "none of us are lumberjacks!"

Having initially taken an interest in what they were doing, Jack decided it was still too hot in the sun and took shelter in the shade provided by a large rock, where he stretched out and dozed.

"Is there any bottled water left?" queried Freddie, wiping the sweat from his brow.

"I'll get it," said Harper. "I put six of them in the water to keep them cool."

The children sat beside Jack in the shade, sipping the water. Harper fetched Jack's bowl, and he also enjoyed a long drink before dog napping again.

Conscious of the time, Freddie reluctantly stood up. It was pleasant just sitting on the beach, listening to the splashing of the water against the rocks and the cry of the gulls overhead.

"We have to get on with this," he said. "I'm guessing the pirates won't return until dark, but we can't be sure exactly when."

150

"We need the ropes from *Swiftwater*," said Noz.

Freddie went over to the boat and untied the painter and stern mooring line. There was also a coil of rope stowed in the bow. He dropped them onto the sand. "Here we are. Hopefully, that's plenty."

"We need to tie one around the bottom of the trunk," responded Noz. "Can one of you seafarers, Freddie or Josh, do that, as it has to be secure? I'm hopeless with knots."

Freddie picked up the painter. "I think a clove hitch is the best knot to use."

"Sounds good," said Noz. "Yes, use one of those clove things."

"Clove hitch," Freddie said with a grin.

He removed his shirt and jumped into the water, wrapping the rope several times around the trunk before tying it tightly. "There, that won't slip."

"Now, all together," said Noz. "Roll the trunk into the water, being careful you don't catch your fingers."

"Hurrah!" they cheered as the tree smoothly entered the channel. The rest of the boys took off their shirts and jumped in after it. Jack, who had been roused from his dog nap by the excited cheering of the children, soon joined them.

As Noz had said, manoeuvring their makeshift blockade was surprisingly easy once the water supported its weight.

Harper stood on the beach smiling at the boys' **antics** and said, "If you place it up tight against the port side rocks you lumberjacks, we can use the rope to swing it across and close the channel off when needed."

151

"Pass that other rope," shouted Freddie. "The painter alone isn't long enough to reach the shore."

Harper threw him the stern mooring line, and he joined it to the painter with a reef knot.

When they had finished setting up the blockade, Josh put the hurricane lamp in place, securing it in a cleft in the rock on the port side of the safe channel.

"What next?" said Leo.

"We should gather some big rocks and boulders. Once *Windchaser* is safely in, we can drop them into the channel. If our pirates get past the blockade, they will make another line of defence," suggested Freddie. "It won't stop them swimming in, but it will make things pretty difficult for them, at least!"

"I agree," said Josh. "Let's stack these boulders on the rock shelves. Rolling them off into the water when the time comes will be easy."

Once they completed everything, they sat back to admire their handiwork.

"*Bon*-good," said Josh with satisfaction. "Now, we need to change out of our wet things."

"Then it's time to eat," declared Freddie. "We don't know when we'll get another chance, and things could get hectic around here pretty soon."

Already, the sun was disappearing, and late afternoon had given way to evening as the Six returned up the path towards their camp.

"I'd better get off to my lookout point, Captain," said Leo. "It won't be all that long before dark."

"I'm only the captain when we're sailing," said Freddie.

Leo grinned. "I know that," he said cheerfully, "but I've sort of got into the habit."

Jack ran ahead and greeted them at the top with his tail wagging, like they were long-lost friends.

Freddie rubbed his ears. "You silly old thing," he said affectionately, "anyone would think we've been gone for hours. Are you hungry, Jack?"

"I am," said Noz, predictably.

Harper distributed the food and drink, not forgetting Jack, and the Secret Six sat and munched while discussing their plans.

"The last thing to do is set a hurricane lamp on the triangle rock and the northern castle, and we're done," said Josh.

"Then all we can do is wait," said Freddie.

Chapter Twenty-Two

Night Passage

"I'll set the lamp on the northern castle," said Harper, "as I've already checked it out, and it involves a bit of climbing. I'm probably the best one to do that." Leo looked towards his sister. "You can say that again. I'll never forget that **perilous** climb you made in Cornwall to rescue us!"

Harper laughed, but she had been very frightened at the time.

"You take this," said Freddie.

Harper took the **proffered** lamp, shook it, and looked concerned. "There's not much oil in it," she reported. "It must have leaked out back at the cave. The lamps were lying on the ground, and there was a strong smell of paraffin was in the air."

Freddie searched amongst the equipment and found the small container of oil the Cooper girls had thoughtfully provided.

"You'd better take this," he said. "It isn't much, but it's all we have."

She took it and put it in her backpack along with the lamp.

"Here, Leo," said Freddie, handing him the last of the lamps. "And take these matches. You can strike them on a rock; no matchbox is needed."

"Aye, aye, Captain," he answered.

"Harper. You'll need some matches, too."

155

He checked his watch. "It's now 19:45 hours, and we expect *Windchaser* at 20:30 hours, so we need the lamps lit at 20:25. That gives us just over half an hour to get everything ready. Okay, everyone?"

"I've got butterflies in my stomach," said Leo, "and I'm feeling quite nervous."

Freddie sympathetically squeezed his arm. "I think we all are," he responded, "but remember, we're doing this for the Coopers, and we are all together."

"The Secret Six!" declared Josh.

"The Secret Six!" affirmed the others, their voices ringing in the still air.

"Up and down, Cooperstown!" called out Leo as he made his way further up the track towards his landmark rock. "Left to right, pirates in sight!"

"Good luck," said Freddie as they disappeared from view.

Josh took hold of Jack's collar. "I don't think you'd better go with Harper this time, Jack. You'll be safer on the beach with us."

"That just leaves us now," said Freddie. "We'd better go down and get ready to light our lamp. Who's volunteering for that?"

"I'll do it," replied Josh, "if you and Noz will watch for Leo's signal."

✳✳✳

Climbing the navigation rock proved surprisingly easy, as rough cuts resembling steps had formed from the collapsed portion of the rock.

On one side was the steep drop into the valley, and the ruins of the northern castle could be seen in the distance.

Leo felt quite safe if he kept away from the edge and stayed where it was flat. He didn't have a head for heights, so was relieved that he didn't have to climb the castle. From where he was stationed, he couldn't see his sister, but he knew that she was more than capable, would find a safe way up, and would see his signal when the time came.

✳✳✳

With her backpack containing the hurricane lamp, Harper set off towards the castle ruins perched high on the rocks overlooking the sea. It was a tough climb, but she knew exactly what to do.

As she approached the ancient stones, she could feel the excitement inside her. The ruins were like a puzzle, but she had climbed similar puzzles many times before.

The sun had begun to set, casting long shadows across the landscape, and she knew she had to hurry. She skillfully scaled the walls, her fingers and toes finding the perfect holds in the weathered stones. With each step, she felt the cool evening breeze on her face. Harper was strong and knew that her recently found friends, Captain Summer and First Mate Scarlett in *Windchaser,* depended on her, which gave her the determination to press on.

Finally, she reached the top and carefully unpacked the hurricane lamp, setting it firmly in place and surrounding it with small rocks to keep it secure.

Then she sat and gazed toward the rock in the distance where Leo was on watch.

She was waiting for his signal. Would it be friends or pirates? She hoped very much that it would be the twin girls.

✻✻✻

Freddie, Josh and Noz stood in the cove, patiently awaiting Leo's signal.

Having sniffed around, Jack had yet to find any fresh smells and was bored by the proceedings. So he jumped over the transom of *Swiftwater,* curled up and went to sleep.

"It's nearly time," commented Josh. "*Windchaser* should be with us any minute if they're not late."

"I wouldn't worry about that," Freddie exclaimed. "If there is any delay, it won't be their fault!"

"It's quite dark now," said Noz. "Don't boats on the water at night have to show a light?"

"They certainly do," responded Freddie. "Can you imagine if they were sailing and motoring all over the place in the dark without lighting? They'd be crashing into each other!"

"So, *Windchaser* will have lights?" asked Noz.

"I heard what Captain Summer said to Scarlett about sailing at night," replied Freddie. "She's far too sensible to take their boat out on the water after dark without the proper lighting."

"Well, at least we should be able to see them in time," answered Noz.

"Unless it's the pirates, of course," responded Freddie, "but I have a feeling they won't be bothering with the rules of the water."

"Leo is signalling," shouted Noz excitedly. "I can see the lamp moving!"

✳✳✳

Summer laid a finger to her lips. "Shhh," she said. "We must be as quiet as possible." She opened the bedroom window and swung her leg over the sill. "Come on."

"You know I don't like climbing," protested Scarlett, "so please don't rush me."

"We've done this lots of times," answered Summer. "You'll be fine. But we have to get a move on if we're to get to Shadowmere Island by 20:30 hours."

She took hold of the tree branch in front of her and climbed to the ground below.

Scarlett slowly followed, to join her sister in the garden.

"I wish I had my woolly hat," said Summer. "I do miss it."

"It *was* good of you, though, to give it to Harper," Scarlett responded. "I was surprised by that. You must like her a lot."

"She—they—all of them—are different from any others I've ever known," responded Summer. "I don't know what it is. Just that they're different, and that will have to do!" She sounded almost cross at being unable to figure it out, and Scarlett decided it was best to keep quiet.

Summer looked back at the house. The lights were on in the downstairs living room and the television was flickering away.

"Mum and Dad won't hear a thing," she said as they went to the bottom of the garden and into the old boathouse where *Windchaser* was waiting.

They pushed their boat outside into the M*ere*, **stepped** the mast and hoisted the sail before navigating into the darkness.

The twins were not yet in their teens, but possessed an **insatiable** thirst for adventure. On this night aboard their little boat *Windchaser*, setting sail towards Shadowmere Island, their youthful faces were illuminated only by the glow of the lantern hanging at the bow of their vessel.

Summer was at the helm, her eyes scanning the inky waters ahead. She wore a weathered leather jacket, giving her an air of authority. Her freckled face held a determined look as she gripped the tiller, guiding their craft through the undulating waves.

Scarlett was perched in the dinghy's bow. She wore a tattered, oversized navy blue **pea coat**, a hand-me-down from her grandfather, who had once sailed the seven seas. It was one of her prized possessions.

Now, her eyes were wide open, darting around as she scanned the darkness for signs of Jamie Jenkins. There was a sense of urgency. He and his mate would no doubt be **en route**, their more powerful motorboat probably slicing through the water with ill intent at that very moment.

Summer and Scarlett exchanged a knowing glance, as Scarlett adjusted the sail, harnessing the wind to propel them forward. The race against time had begun, and their young hearts beat with the excitement of adventure. Shadowmere Island could be seen in the distance, and they made speed as they were running before the wind and, therefore, did not need to tack.

"Keep an eye out for the bad guys," said Captain Summer.

"Aye, aye," responded the first mate dutifully as *Windchaser* ploughed on in the brisk breeze, the gap between the boat and the island narrowing every minute.

"Boat on the starboard bow," cried Scarlett, as the sound of a powerful engine in the distance cut through the stillness of the night.

"Lower the mainsail," commanded Summer, and Scarlett dropped it down, where it hung in folds over the boom.

"Extinguish the bow lantern," continued Summer, and Scarlett quickly opened the glass door and blew it out.

Then they sat in silence, their boat drifting quietly, the only sounds being the gurgle of water against the hull and the throb of the powerboat somewhere ahead.

"It's got to be that weasel, Jamie Jenkins. Who else would head for our island in the dark? I hope he didn't spot us," whispered Scarlett nervously.

"They haven't changed course," responded Summer, "and although they've cut their power, they are still on a northerly bearing towards the island, so I don't think they have."

"What do we do?" asked Scarlett. "They're going to be at the island before us. I hope the *Swiftwater* crew are well-prepared."

"Hoist the mainsail," responded Summer, "Although it goes against all my seamanship, we'll run without our lamp. They'll never spot us in the dark."

Soon, Windchaser was back on course, propelled rapidly along by the breeze.

"There they are," breathed Scarlett softly from her position in the bow, "five hundred metres south of the channel. They aren't carrying navigation lights either, and it looks like they're riding at anchor."

Men's voices carried clearly across the water, and Summer recognised that of the tweedy man.

They appeared to be arguing as their voices were raised and angry and could be heard from within the boat's cabin.

"I've got an idea," said Summer urgently. "Lower the mainsail, and we'll use the oars to get closer." Scarlett **complied** and reefed it around the boom.

"Don't bother doing that," said Summer. "You'll have to raise it pretty quickly in a few minutes."

They rowed silently until the powerboat was about twenty metres ahead.

"Lower the anchor," said Summer, "but make sure you do it quietly."

"Whatever are you up to?" implored Scarlett as she lowered it over the side and into the water, feeling the rope go slack as it touched the bottom.

"Don't worry," responded her twin, "it will be fine. Just be ready to raise it and the sail because we'll have to make a quick getaway when I return!" With that, she slipped off her coat and top clothes, grabbed a coiled rope from under the transom, and slipped over the side of the boat and into the black water.

Scarlett uneasily waited in the boat, scanning the water. There was no sight or sound of Summer, but the men could still be heard from the boat ahead.

Some minutes passed before Summer appeared at the side of the boat as quietly as she had left. "Give me a hand," she said, breathing heavily. "I've been swimming hard."

Scarlett helped pull Summer into the boat, where she fell into the bottom, shaking violently.

"Are you okay? What's happened?" cried Scarlett anxiously. Then she realised that Summer was laughing uncontrollably.

She pulled on her clothes and jacket, still laughing mischievously.

"Quick, anchors aweigh," she said. "Then light the lamp and raise the mainsail."

"Are you sure?" said Scarlett in amazement.

"You'll see," responded Summer.

As soon as the wind filled *Windchaser's* sail, Summer took the helm and steered the boat directly towards the powerboat.

"Ahoy," she shouted as the distance between them closed. "Ahoy on the boat!"

The cabin door of the boat flew open, and Jenkins and the tweedy man appeared on deck.

Summer held her course until the last moment before putting the helm hard over to prevent a collision.

"Gybo!" she shouted gleefully and let fly the sheet, causing the boom to hurtle across from port to starboard and the sail to flap wildly, brushing so close to the tweedy man that it almost knocked him overboard, causing him to duck and shout out furiously.

"Get that sail taut," shouted Summer as they passed close by the bow of the powerboat, "We're steering our course directly to Shadowmere Island, full speed ahead!"

Scarlett obeyed, but was bemused by what had happened. Had Summer lost her wits?

Chapter Twenty-Three

The Pirates

"Leo is signalling," shouted Noz excitedly. "I can see the lamp moving!"

"Cooperstown or pirates in sight," queried Freddie, with a slight waver in his voice.

"Up and down!" declared Josh. "It's *Windchaser.*"

"Thank goodness for that," said Freddie with relief. "Let's get our hurricane lamp lit."

"*Tout suite*—immediately," responded Josh as he waded into the water and lit the last channel marker. Harper had already seen Leo's signal and lit the wick of her lamp with a steady hand. A warm, flickering glow filled it—the lamp's glass panes casting shadows in the dark.

As she turned the wick up, the light intensified, shining like a beacon and cutting through the darkness. Her heart swelled with satisfaction as she looked out over the expanse of the *Mere*. She knew *Windchaser* would see the lights, and the Coopers could now safely navigate through the channel and into the cove.

And at that very moment, the lamp spluttered and went out, plunging the castle into darkness.

Meanwhile, Leo, confident that Freddie had seen his signal from his position on the beach, as had Harper atop the north castle, set his lamp down where it

165

would be visible across the water.

✳✳✳

"I can't see a thing," said Summer. "Where are our lamps?"

"I can't see them," responded Scarlett, "and we're almost at the entrance to the channel. If the *Swiftwater* crew doesn't light us up soon, we'll have to abort!"

"Steady as she goes," said Summer, "keep your eyes peeled for the markers."

"We don't have a lot of safe water ahead of us," responded Scarlett. "We're already in unknown territory where we've never dared venture before. There's only a few hundred metres, and then we'll have to go about before it's too late, or *Windchaser* will **founder** on the rocks!"

Just as it seemed they would have to abort, two lamps burst into light ahead of them.

"There, Captain. Two of them. One in the channel and one up on the triangle rock."

"There are meant to be three," said Summer. "What about the north castle? We should take our bearing from that and also the rock."

"I can't see a third," said Scarlett. "Perhaps something has gone wrong?"

"Well, whatever it is, I won't risk taking *Windchaser* in unless I'm certain," responded Summer. "I can't see the castle in the dark."

✳✳✳

When her hurricane lamp failed, for just a moment, Harper was at a loss to know what to do. The

166

seriousness of the situation hit her like a blow. It was **imperative** that the girls could line up the triangle rock with the castle on which she was standing. And at that moment, the castle was in absolute blackness. Then she thought of the tin of spare oil. That was the solution!

Picking up the lamp, her fingers grasped the screw filler cap. If she could put some oil in, then all would be well. Except that try as she might, the cap would not unscrew. It was rusted solid.

With no time to waste, she frantically surveyed her surroundings in search of a solution to the impending crisis.

The pirates were out there somewhere, and if they came across *Windchaser* stranded outside the safe channel, that would be disastrous. Pitting sail against a motorboat was a non-contest. And, of course, the risk of the girls running aground or onto the hidden rocks in their boat was a real danger.

✳✳✳

"Ready to go about," called out Summer. Their boat had run out of safe space, and it was time to take her away from the dangerous rocks.

"Wait!" shouted Scarlett excitedly. "There's the third light up on the castle now."

Perched atop the island, the castle ruins stood boldly against the night sky with flames dancing wildly at its top. Scarlett couldn't contain her excitement. "It's like a massive bonfire!"

"It's not a hurricane lamp, that's for sure," responded Summer, as great flames were leaping upwards, reaching into the blackness of the sky.

"It looks like they've set the entire castle on fire!" said Scarlett.

"No matter, that will do us," replied Summer as she lined up the bow of their boat with the lamp on the marker rock and the inferno raging at the top of the castle.

"Lower the mainsail," she called, and Scarlett obediently pulled it down, wrapping it loosely around the boom.

"Stand by with the oar," said Summer, "and be ready to fend us off from any rocks."

With careful precision, she steered their vessel through the narrow channel, keeping a watchful eye on the port side hurricane lamp, ensuring they stayed well to starboard.

"Rocks on the port side," called out Scarlett, pushing the boat away with the oar. "And there are the *Swiftwater* boys!" she shouted eagerly, spotting them on the beach.

Summer leaned in closer to Scarlett, her voice tinged with concern. "I don't want to alarm you, First Mate Scarlett, but I can hear the powerboat, and it's getting close!"

✱✱✱

Freddie, Josh and Noz were staring at the flames licking around the **castellated** top of the castle.

"What's happened?" exclaimed Josh. "That fire is never a hurricane lamp!"

"Something has gone wrong," said Freddie. "We need to make sure Harper is okay."

"It's worked anyway," said Noz. "Look, here comes *Windchaser.*"

"Sorry, Noz, I know you don't like the climb," said Freddie, "but you'll have to get Leo and check that Harper hasn't been hurt. Josh and I have to put the barricade in place once the girls have entered the cove."

Noz moved off up the dreaded cliff path while Freddie dove into the water and swam out to the hurricane lamp positioned by the starboard rock wall. He held it high, waving it from side to side, and *Windchaser* responded by signalling back with its bow lamp.

"They're right on course," said Freddie, "but there's a big powerboat behind them!"

"It's the pirates!" exclaimed Josh.

Chapter Twenty-Four

Shipwrecked

"It looks like they're meeting up with those little monsters I locked in the cave."

Jamie Jenkins scowled as he looked through the porthole at *Windchaser,* making its way towards Shadowmere Island with a fair wind behind it.

"This is getting worse," retorted Black Bart. "That now makes seven kids we have to deal with!"

"Seven kids and a vicious dog," replied Jenkins.

"If they know the way into the cove," said Bart, "we can just follow them in."

"They must have had sight of the chart," responded Jenkins. "They've always left their boat at anchor and swam to the island in the past, the same as I have had to."

"Well, whatever. As soon as these clouds clear, we need to be up high to see the full moon, and no bunch of kids will stop me. This island is mine, and I want whatever Jack Swiftwater has hidden here. *And* I have a score to settle with those girls. They almost tipped me overboard with their amateur boat handling!"

"Technically, the island isn't yours yet," pointed out Jenkins. "Not 'till the papers are signed tomorrow. And having seen the girls many times on the water, I would say it wasn't carelessness. They deliberately steered their boat at us!"

171

Black Bartholomew Worthington **huffed** loudly as he climbed the **companionway** out of the cabin.

"Let's just get after them," he said. "We'll stand off until they enter the passage to the cove, then we'll show them what damage a powerboat can do to a little sailboat!"

He grinned **maliciously**, and it wasn't a pleasant sight.

"Surely you aren't going to run them down?" said Jamie Jenkins fearfully.

Black Bart pressed the engine's starter button and opened the throttle to full speed.

But instead of the powerful twin outboard engines roaring into life, they backfired with a loud bang, followed by a screeching sound, before both shuddered to a stop. Black Bart's face was as dark as thunder in the silence that followed.

"If this is the work of those twin brats…" he said **ominously**.

Stripping off his top clothes, he lowered himself over the stern of the boat and into the water to check the engines. When he eventually clambered back on board, his face was twisted in anger.

He threw a shredded rope onto the deck.

"Give me a towel, you idiot," he said, "don't just stand there!"

Jamie passed it to him, and he wiped himself dry before speaking.

"One engine is busted and needs some serious repair work. I don't know about the other. That halyard was wrapped around both the propellors, and it didn't get there by itself. No wonder something went bang."

He **tentatively** pressed the starter button, and the

172

single engine rattled and clanked as it slowly turned over before roaring into life.

Worthington smiled unpleasantly. "Now we go and get them," he said.

Even with one engine, the boat's power was so much greater than *Windchaser's* that it quickly caught up with it.

"Pass me that chart," he said. "Does it show how to avoid the underwater rocks and shallows?"

Jamie Jenkins grudgingly passed it over. He hadn't been paid anything for his work so far, and he didn't altogether trust his companion. So far, he hadn't disclosed all the clues leading to the treasure, and he was determined not to do that until he was sure.

Black Bart looked at the drawing that Harper had prepared.

"Ok, so we line up that far castle with this triangular rock, and that's our course," he stated confidently. He looked up from the chart. "It's all very well," he shouted angrily, "but I can't see the castle or the rock in the dark."

"Why don't we follow the twin girls in?" suggested Jenkins. "Instead of ramming them as you suggested, let's follow them into the cove."

Black Bart snorted but didn't have a better idea, so he unwillingly agreed.

"But once we're inside…" he said threateningly, leaving no doubt about his intentions.

He opened the throttle wide, and as he did so, a light appeared inside the cove and then another on top of the triangle rock, which was now visible in the flickering flame.

"They've got this set up nicely," he grunted as he slowed the engine. "Let's see if they light up the castle, too. If they do, we won't need the girls. We'll power straight in!"

"They seem to have slowed right down," said Jenkins. "What are they waiting for?"

"What do you think, you idiot? The third light, of course."

"They're taking their time, if you ask me," said Jamie.

"No one is asking you anything," was the reply.

Then, the castle lit up as a great blaze erupted on top of it, the flames dancing up into the night sky.

"And there we are," said Black Bart Worthington with satisfaction. "Our route into the cove and Captain Jack's treasure!"

As *Windchaser* slipped into the channel, he opened the throttle. Had both engines been working, he would have caught up with the sailing boat in no time. But with just one engine, although still much faster, it wasn't quite fast enough and was several minutes behind.

Windchaser glided into the cove, and Scarlett leapt over the side.

Summer raised the rudder, and without **impediment**, the boat settled into the sand as it beached.

Freddie and Josh took hold of the bow, and together with the first mate, they pulled it further up, away from the water's edge.

Alerted by the noise, Jack jumped out of *Swiftwater* and ran down to see what was happening. He was delighted to see Summer and Scarlett again and wagged his tail furiously, his bright eyes staring at them intently.

Both girls made a fuss of him, and his tail wagged even harder.

"Quick," said Josh, "we've set up a blockade for the pirates, and we must get it in place now as they're right on your heels!"

"Pirates?" queried Scarlett.

"That's what we've been calling that Jamie Jenkins and the tweedy man," responded Freddie.

"Where's the blockade?" said Summer. "I can't see anything."

Freddie smiled. "Watch," he said. "Would you mind taking hold of Jack, or he might jump into the water? It could be dangerous for him."

Summer held onto him, while Freddie and Josh took hold of *Swiftwater's* painter and the halyard draped along the edge of the rock wall. Together, they heaved on it with all their strength, and the tree they had worked so hard preparing floated slowly across the mouth of the channel, wedging itself in the cliff face and completely blocking access to the cove.

"Now the rocks!" shouted Josh, and he and Freddie rolled the boulders into the *Mere,* where they disappeared under the surface with a great splash.

"That was clever thinking," said Summer in admiration.

"I'd like to see the pirates get their boat through now," said Freddie with satisfaction.

He blew out his lamp and noted with approval that Leo on the triangle rock had done the same. All that was left of the markers into the bay was the fading red embers atop the castle.

"Where's Harper," said Summer. "And your other crew?"

"Oh, goodness," responded Josh, "we sent Noz to check on her. As you saw, she started a bit of a blaze up there. Come on!"

Just then, there was an enormous splintering sound, and they turned round in time to see the powerboat smash into their blockade.

"The fools," said Freddie, "what did they think they were doing? They were going much too fast!"

"We can't just leave them," said Josh. "They might be injured and drown."

Summer and Scarlett looked amazed. "But they're pirates," they chorused.

"We shouldn't help them!" pleaded Scarlett.

Freddie ignored the plea and ran into the water. As he did so, Jack stood at the edge and barked ferociously. He recognised the smell of the weasel man, and he didn't like him one little bit.

Freddie saw Jenkins and the tweedy man surface and begin to swim for the shore.

"They're okay, they're swimming," he shouted. "Now run!"

And with that, the two girls, along with Freddie and Josh, ran up the stony cliff path toward the northern castle.

Jack overtook them and waited with Harper, Leo, and Noz, who were on their way down.

"We've got to get to the top," panted Scarlett. "The pirates have just sunk their boat and will be ashore at any moment!"

"Don't tell me I've got to climb up again!" said Noz. "I'm only just recovering from the first time!"

"Come on," said Freddie, "we've got a camp of sorts up here where they won't find us. And the least we can do is offer you a drink and something to eat after all the excitement. You only just got into the cove before the pirates. Another couple of minutes, and they would have cut you off."

"We're all right," said Summer. "Are you okay, Harper? What's with the bonfire on the castle roof?"

Harper smiled. "I'm fine. It's just that my lamp ran out of fuel, and I couldn't refill it. So I gathered a pile of dead branches, leaves and twigs, poured the paraffin on it and lit it. It wasn't easy. But once it started, it roared up in a huge blaze, catching light to everything around it!"

Summer laughed. "At least you made sure the channel was lit up for us," she said.

"I should think everyone could see it as far out as Cooperstown," laughed Josh.

"I tried to take care it was safe," explained Harper, "and surrounded it with big rocks and cleared the area as best I could to make sure it wouldn't spread. I had a horrible vision of the whole island catching fire, but I didn't want to waste any time. I knew you would be waiting for my signal."

"It was quick thinking," congratulated Freddie.

"I'm glad you and Scarlett made it safely here," said Harper softly.

"I see you still haven't quite got the hang of the hat," said Summer. "Hold on."

She adjusted Harper's **coveted** red woollen hat backwards on her head. "That's better. *Now* you've got the buccaneer look," she laughed.

177

"Food?" Scarlett reminded them. "Summer and I missed our supper to get here, so we are hungry."

"I'm hungry, too," said Noz.

"Don't worry," responded Harper. "We won't leave you out." She turned to Summer. "We need a whole stack of food just for Noz!" she said. "He's forever hungry and on the lookout for something to eat."

"Talking of lookouts," said Josh, "We'd better post one to keep an eye out for the scurvy pirates. It won't take them long to recover and get to the top of the island for the full moon."

"Wrecking their boat would have slowed them down, anyway," remarked Leo, "and make them think twice about taking on the Secret Six."

"Secret Six?" said Scarlett. "Is that what you call yourselves?"

"Oops," said Leo. "I shouldn't have said that. I forgot you aren't one of us."

"Hold on," said Freddie. "Didn't we all sign the Ship's Articles? Didn't we all agree to be honest and fair with each other? And what about **camaraderie**?" He turned to Summer and Scarlett. "Having shaken hands and signed our names in blood, you aren't just one of us; you are part of us, and we are a part of you!"

Leo looked ashamed. "I didn't mean…"

Scarlet shoved him gently on the arm. "It's okay, Leo," she said, "I know what you meant. And thanks for all you've done. We couldn't have done any of this without you."

She glanced at Summer, and an unspoken twin's message passed between them.

"It's true," replied Summer. "Your secret is safe with

us. *Windchaser* and *Swiftwater* forever!"
And Jack barked and wagged his tail before trotting over to Summer and curling up beside her.

✳✳✳

The men, dubbed 'pirates' by Captain Freddie and the crew, were jubilant as they powered into the channel towards the cove.

Windchaser had already navigated the narrow corridor and was safely on the beach. The light on the north castle and the one on the triangular rock were aligned, and the channel was clear for the powerboat that was racing as fast as its single engine would take it.

That was before the tree swung across the inlet and blocked their passage.

With relentless momentum and no means of halting its course, the boat thundered headlong into the blockade, producing an earth-shattering collision that pulverised the bow as if it were constructed of flimsy cardboard.

The pirates leapt overboard in panic as the boat **listed** to one side before, little by little, sliding under the water and disappearing from view.

Both men surfaced in a state of shock, unsure what had happened. Then the castle blaze subdued, the triangular light was extinguished, and they were left swimming in the darkness.

Chapter Twenty-Five

Shadow of the Moon

"Read out the clue to remind us of what we're looking for, Harper," said Freddie.

They were all stood on the island's highest point between the two castles, waiting for the full moon to disclose the secrets the island had kept for hundreds of years.

Harper took out the crumpled paper and read it aloud.

Between the castles, when the moon is full at ten, take the narrow and safe way.

Josh checked his watch. "It's almost ten o'clock now," he said.

"Shouldn't we say 22:00?" responded Leo.

"As long as we all know what we mean," said Freddie. "But I agree, especially on board our boat, we should use the twenty-four-hour clock."

"Come on, you boys," interrupted Summer. "Let's concentrate on what's going to happen rather than how we say it!"

Harper smiled. She was glad to have the girls on the adventure with her.

"It's almost time," reported Freddie, staring down into the valley.

The moon was high; the clouds had moved on as if on demand, and the full moon, now shining brightly, cast long silhouettes across the rocks littering the ground below them.

Gathered on the path between the castles, they wondered how the convergence of moon and time would reveal the entrance they had to take.

And then, at the precise time, the moonbeam hit a large, pointed edifice in the foreground, and the shadow it generated, like an **elongated** arrow, stretched across the valley floor until it stopped at a pile of rocks at the base of the cliff.

"That's it," breathed Summer. "That's where the treasure is hidden!"

"I can hardly believe it," responded Scarlett. "After all these centuries!"

They hastened down the steep path into the valley and made their way to the pile of rocks.

Jack sniffed at them inquisitively before looking back at the children, waiting for a command.

"Sorry, Jack," said Freddie. "I'm not sure where we go from here."

"There's no entrance," said Leo in disappointment.

"Perhaps it's this one?" said Scarlett, pointing to an opening to the side of the rock pile. "It looks accessible and easy to get into."

"But that's not what the clue said," responded Josh. "It was quite clear. Choose the narrow way."

"But there isn't a way at all," replied Scarlett, "narrow or otherwise, other than this passage. It's this one or nothing."

"Perhaps the rocks have worn over the years, so the shadow didn't fall in the right place?" queried Leo.

"Noz, do you remember the secret door at Smugglers' Cove?" said Freddie.

"I absolutely do," responded Noz. "It trapped us in

the tunnel, and I thought we would all drown!" [1]

He paused for a moment. "Ah, I see what you mean. Is there a chance that there's a secret entrance here?" Because his hobby was magic tricks, Noz was very good at finding hidden mysteries.

He took off his glasses and polished them on his shirt, and while the Cooper girls looked on in amazement, he crouched down by the pile of rocks, running his hand over their surface and examining each one in detail.

"That is crafty," he said as the others crowded around him. "There's not a secret door *in* the rocks," he said. "The rocks *are* the door. Look!" He put his shoulder to it, pushed, and it moved slightly. "I'm not surprised it doesn't easily give up its secrets," he continued. "After centuries of rain pouring down on it, it will be a bit **silted** up."

The others lent a hand, leaning against the stubborn rock until, with a scraping sound and a cloud of dust, it swivelled inwards, exposing a small entrance. What secrets and wonders awaited? The combination of darkness and silence lent an air of both **trepidation** and excitement as each **contemplated** the journey into the heart of the cave.

"It's a bit dark," said Harper.

"That's to be expected," said Freddie. "But we've got a hurricane lamp. I won't light it until we get further into the tunnel in case the pirates see the reflection." He got down on all fours and crawled into the darkness, taking the lamp with him.

"I'm not sure I like confined spaces," said Scarlett

[1] The Adventure at Smugglers' Cove

uncertainly.

"I don't exactly love them," said Harper, "so we'll keep together."

Freddie's voice floated hollowly out of the tunnel. "The air is fresh, so there must be an inlet somewhere, but I'm afraid we'll have to crawl for a bit. I can't yet see where the passage opens up."

Harper and Scarlett looked at each other wide-eyed, and Harper took her hand.

"We Secret Six have a saying. All of us or none of us. A bit like the Three Musketeers! We all stick together, in other words."

And she led the way, with Scarlett and Summer following closely behind.

The tunnel roof seemed to press down on them as they went, creating a **claustrophobic** feeling, but they kept moving onwards into the heart of the cave system, encouraged by the thought of finding the long-lost treasure of poor William Cooper. How exciting to be able to restore it to its rightful owners! Seeing Harper enter the darkness, Jack went in behind, wagging his tail in anticipation of what lay ahead.

The others followed, with Noz coming last. He moved the rock door back into position behind him, wondering whether they would be able to open it again from the inside. He took off his spectacles and polished them furiously, keeping his fear to himself so as not to alarm the others.

There was a spark of light as Freddie struck a match and lit the lamp, creating an almost hypnotic flicker that seemed to draw them further into its depths.

"It opens up ahead," he called back, "and then you

can stand. It's huge!"

"Thank goodness for that," said Summer. "My knees are getting sore."

After what seemed a long time, they rounded a bend in the tunnel, and as Freddie had said, the cave dramatically opened into a vast cathedral-like space. They stood together to catch their breath, wondering what lay ahead.

Jack made the most of the stop, visiting each of the children for a bit of fuss before sitting to see what would happen next.

Chapter Twenty-Six

Labyrinth

Black Bart was a stranger to exercise and was panting heavily by the time he had climbed to the high point on the island.

He was in a furious mood, having almost been catapulted into the water by the *Windchaser* girls, having his boat engines **sabotaged**, and then, the final **catastrophe**, having his boat wrecked and having to abandon ship!

"When we've located the treasure," he said, "we'll deal with all those kids. And as for *their* boats, they won't be sailing in them again!" And he smiled wickedly.

Jamie Jenkins was a crook, as dishonest a man as you could hope to meet. All he wanted was money—lots and lots of it—and a life living in luxury. He plodded along behind Black Bart, dreaming of what goodies he would buy with his share of Swiftwater Jack's treasure.

"What time is it?"

"It's a couple of minutes past ten," replied Jamie.

"It's about time you showed me the clue," ordered Black Bart. "That's what I'm paying you for."

Jenkins handed it over. "It says that the moon's light will reveal where the treasure is at ten," he said.

"I can read," snapped Black Bart. A shadow was visible as they looked down the valley, pointing at a large rock cave with a wide opening.

"It says to take the safe way, the broad path," he said. "So let's do that. Where's the torch?"

Jamie Jenkins handed it over, and the two went down into the valley where the children had ventured just minutes before.

✳✳✳

In the cave, the hurricane lamp carried by Freddie was a beacon of hope for the adventurous children. At times, the oppressive darkness threatened to swallow them whole, and the echoes of their footsteps bouncing off the cavern walls created an eerie ambience.

But the light was also their guide through the uneven terrain of jagged rocks and hidden crevices. It created a sense of security in the otherwise intimidating environment.

The limited range of the lamp's flickering light intensified the suspense of the treasure hunt, the shadows cast by the flame casting elongated shadows that danced and played tricks on their imaginations.

"Just think," whispered Summer, "Captain Jack walked these very tunnels hundreds of years ago!"

"I wonder if he was alone?" queried Harper. "I don't think he would have taken anyone into his confidence, do you?"

"If he did, the treasure has probably gone by now," said Josh.

"Don't say that!" said Summer sharply.

"I can't imagine being alone underground," said Scarlett, quickly changing the subject. She didn't like cross words between friends. "So I'm glad we're all here, and little Jack too!"

Hearing his name, Jack wagged his tail. He was happy so long as he was with his children.

"It's creepy enough being with everyone," said Leo. "It would be so scary alone."

"We're explorers in an uncharted world," said Noz.

"Come on, you lot, what's keeping you!" shouted Freddie, who was ahead of them. "I can see light ahead."

"What exactly are we looking for, now that we're here?" asked Josh.

"I've no idea," responded Freddie, "other than it's a treasure. But we'll probably recognise it when we see it."

The children continued onwards until Jack, who had been contentedly trotting beside Harper, suddenly dashed ahead and disappeared from view in the cave system.

The children hurried to catch up with him, being careful not to trip on the uneven floor, and as they rounded the corner, what they saw caused them to come to a standstill.

***

"So, Einstein, what do we do next?"

Black Bart was livid, hot and tired. Jamie Jenkins and he had been walking around in circles for the past thirty minutes, always returning to the same place they started from.

Having entered the cave system by what they thought was a straightforward, easy route, they had turned off at various underground crossroads and were now unable to find the exit. They were totally lost, deep underground.

And to make matters worse, the battery in their torch was rapidly running out, the light from it getting dimmer.

"Don't blame me," whimpered Jenkins. "My job was to find a route to the island and then show you where the treasure is. I've done that. You can't blame me for getting lost in a labyrinth of tunnels."

Then, the torch flickered one last time before extinguishing, leaving the two would-be treasure seekers in complete darkness.

Chapter Twenty-Seven

The Treasure Seekers

"I think we've found it!" shouted Freddie.

As they turned the corner, the children's eyes widened in amazement. There, illuminated by a faint light filtering in from the cave roof high above and reinforced by the yellow glow of their lamp, was a big wooden chest. It stood against the wall where it seemed it had always been, waiting patiently to be discovered.

And little Jack was busy examining it, his brown eyes sparkling in the light.

It was truly a sight to behold for the young treasure seekers. Its wood was aged and worn, with carvings that hinted at the passage of time. Iron hinges, rusted and ornate, held the chest together, a relic from the distant past.

"Is this it?" asked Summer, her voice shaking. "Can this really be Captain Jack's lost fortune?"

"No, it's William Cooper's lost fortune," said Freddie. "Jack Swiftwater stole it, but it belongs to you now. Go on, open it."

The girls stood back, afraid of what they might find. What if the chest were empty, and the treasure gone, as Leo had said? The disappointment would be too much after all the excitement and adventure they'd been through.

"Go on," encouraged Harper. "It's only right that you

two have the privilege."

Shaking with excitement, the Cooper twins approached the chest and carefully lifted the lid. And they gasped in awe as they beheld the long-lost treasure of centuries. Glittering jewels of every colour imaginable spilled out, catching the light of the hurricane lamp and scattering prismatic rays across the cave walls. Rubies sparkled like fresh blood, sapphires resembled the depths of the ocean, and emeralds glowed with an otherworldly green.

And there were stacks of gold coins engraved with intricate designs and worn from age, neatly organised within the chest. But the centrepiece of the incredible find was a magnificent crown encrusted with gemstones that shone with an inner fire. It seemed to pulse with its own magic as though it knew the adventures of countless seekers who had sought its riches down the years.

It was too much for the Cooper twins, and they stepped back, their eyes filled with tears.

"Can this be real?" wept Summer. "Can this really be the fortune of William Cooper?"

"I don't believe it," said Scarlett. "It can't be true. Treasure chests and jewels? It's like something out of a story!"

Jack trotted over and sat between Summer and Scarlett, and they leaned down to stroke his floppy ears.

"Good boy, Jack," they said.

"Here's what looks like a letter," said Noz, pushing his glasses up on his nose where they had slipped down, "and some other papers." He handed the yellowing parchments to Summer, who gave them to Harper.

"Would you mind reading them," she pleaded in a shaky voice, "I'm not sure that I can take any more surprises."

She closed the lid of the chest, and she and Scarlett sat on it with their arms around each other.

"One of these papers looks like a deed to Swiftwater Cottage," said Harper. "I only know that because it has the word 'DEED' written in big letters at the top. The other is a deed to this island."

Summer and Scarlett sat in silence, their eyes wide. Harper returned the documents to Summer and opened the letter, reading it silently while the others looked on. "Oh, wow," she exclaimed. "Just listen to this!"

She cleared her throat, holding the parchment nearer to the light of their lamp.

"It's written by Captain Jack Swiftwater," she began;

Should thou chance upon this precious trove, O brave and nameless explorers, then it shall be thine. By virtue of this document, I doth bestow upon thee, as rightful possessor, the said treasure, this island, and all that doth abide upon it unto eternity.

193

I doth confess in most profound contrition for my despicable conduct towards my fellow man, William Cooper, who deemed me his comrade. 'Twas by mine own hand that his demise was wrought and driven by insatiable avarice, I did conceal his opulence within this cave in Whispering Cove.

Yet, my conscience hath laid me low, and thus, as I depart from this mortal realm, I beseech thee, noble seeker, to intercede for my wretched soul, and may divine forgiveness be bestowed upon me by the grace of God.

"It's signed by him and dated," said Harper, "and this big wax seal is on it. There are also three signatures as witnesses. One name I can read says, 'Reverend Jeremiah Thornton.'"

Summer and Scarlett got to their feet, and the Secret Six waited quietly.

"He wasn't totally evil," sniffed Scarlett.

"He was sorry for what he did at the end," replied Summer. "I'm glad he realised the error of his ways. Perhaps that's why he had the Reverend Thornton as a witness?"

"He calls it 'Whispering Cove,'" said Summer. "That must have been the original name for it."

"You named it Smugglers' Cove, Harper," said Scarlett. "So that's what it will always be to us."

"What do we do now?" asked Josh. "It's an enormous trunk."

"We'll have to report this to the proper authorities," responded Noz. He took off his glasses and polished them energetically before waving them in the air. "I don't know much about treasure, except that it has to be at least 300 years old. I've also heard of the

Treasure Act, and I think that a court of some sort decides what happens to it. And as for the Deeds…"

"You'd better keep those documents safe then," warned Leo. "Whoever has the island has everything!"

"These must be what our pirates were hoping to find," said Freddie.

"Does it mean the tweedy man can't buy the island after all?" asked Leo.

"*Je l'espère*—I really hope so," said Josh.

Chapter Twenty-Eight

Captain Swiftwater's Ghost

"You're an idiot!" exploded Black Bart. "We've been wandering in the dark for the past hour and found nothing!"

"We've found the way out," said Jamie Jenkins.

"Found the way out?!" shouted Bart. "I've paid a lot of money to a lot of people to buy this island and get the treasure, and all I've got to show for it is a tour of underground caverns. And in the dark at that!"

"Will I still get my money?" he asked.

Then he ran out of the cave as Black Bart came after him with a look of violence in his eyes.

Straight into the Secret Six and the Cooper girls standing outside.

"Well," said Black Bart, "what have we here?"

Jack's hackles rose, and he growled, ready to launch at both men.

Freddie caught hold of his collar and clipped on his lead to stop him. "Hush, Jack," he cautioned, "keep away from those ruffians."

Jenkins strutted arrogantly up to them, his courage having returned and his hope of making money resurging.

Freddie loosened Jack's lead sufficiently for him to leap forward, and his teeth only just missed nipping Jamie's ankle as the weasel hastily retreated.

"You see?" said Jenkins nervously. "I told you they

had a savage dog!"

"Get out of my way," ordered Black Bart, pushing Jamie Jenkins roughly aside, "let me deal with this." He opened his jacket, showing the pistol stuck in the waistband of his trousers.

"Don't make me use this, kids," he said menacingly, pointing a finger at Jack. "That mongrel will be first if I have to."

"He's not a mongrel," said Harper indignantly. "If you knew anything, you'd know he is a cocker spaniel."

"Harper," warned Leo, "don't argue with him."

The children stepped back, watching Bart nervously. Jamie Jenkins put out his hand, making sure it was nowhere near where Jack could get to it.

"Hand it over; I know you've got it," he demanded.

"What do you mean?" asked Freddie in what he hoped was an innocent-sounding voice.

"Don't waste my time," said Black Bart. "You know exactly what. The deeds to the island."

Freddie glanced at Summer. What could they do? They were in a perilous situation, and it was no time to play the hero.

Noz looked at Leo and nodded **imperceptibly** before speaking to Summer.

"Give him the deeds," he said. "They won't do him any good."

"That's a good boy," responded Jamie Jenkins sneeringly. "Let's have them."

"Let me have the deed to the island," said Noz softly, "and I'll hand it over. You don't want to go anywhere near them."

Summer did as he asked, her eyes glistening.

"Don't worry," he told her, "everything will be okay. I promise." Then he whispered so that only the Cooper girls could hear. "Whatever happens, don't worry, Okay? I'll explain afterwards, but the important thing is that you will be absolutely safe." He held out the paper to Jamie Jenkins.

"I want to see it first," he said. "I don't trust you kids one bit!"

Noz opened it and showed the weasel-faced man and Bart the ancient document with the word 'DEED' at the top.

"That'll do," responded Jenkins. "Gimme it now." Noz handed it over, and Jenkins looked at Black Bart before stuffing it in his pocket for safekeeping.

"Anything else?" he asked Bart.

"Where's the treasure," said Bart. "I know you've found it." His eyes narrowed with greed. "Well?"

"There's something or someone in that cave that stopped us looking. I think it's Captain Jack's ghost! We ran out because we were scared," said Leo.

The rest of the children looked at him in surprise. What was he up to?

Jamie Jenkins stepped away from the cave entrance, his face white with dread.

"I've heard stories about the captain's ghost," he said. "Lots of local people swear they have seen his phantom **Schooner** sailing to the island at night so he can gloat over his treasure!"

"Don't be a fool," responded Black Bart. "There's no such thing. It's just silly superstitious nonsense!" He took out his pistol and pointed it at the children. "I don't know what you're up to, you lot, but get in

199

there now," he ordered. "You too," he added, waving his firearm at Jamie Jenkins. "I don't need you anymore."

The children reluctantly entered the cave Bart pointed them to. The pirates had no idea, but it wasn't the one with the treasure.

Jamie nervously followed, staying close to Freddie and Josh. He believed in ghosts and was afraid.

"Give me that lamp," said Bart gruffly, snatching the hurricane lamp from Freddie's hand. "Matches?" Freddie handed over the box, and Black Bart lit the lamp, the dancing flame lighting up the cave's interior and disclosing the series of tunnels stretching ahead.

It felt like a totally different world, with the flame casting eerie shadows on the uneven walls. Unlike the treasure cave, the walls of this cave were rough and rocky, covered in damp, glistening moss that made it feel like a hidden jungle. Water droplets dripped from the ceiling, making soft, pinging sounds as they hit the ground. It seemed like a spooky adventure movie, with just the right setting for Captain Jack's ghost.

Every step they took echoed back at them, creating eerie sounds that seemed to come from nowhere. The whole place felt like it held secrets. And Leo had one of his own, known only to the Secret Six.

He had a special talent that set him apart from other children his age—he could do ventriloquism, which meant he could make it seem like his voice was coming from anywhere he wanted. But this time, it wasn't for fun; he was about to use it to outsmart the pirates, Black Bart and Jamie Jenkins.

Leo and Noz had exchanged looks outside the cave, and a plan had formed in his mind. He didn't know what Noz had planned, but he was sure something was up.

Black Bart and Jenkins had been determined to get their hands on the treasure that rightfully belonged to Summer and Scarlett. However, it seemed that Bart had now cut Jenkins adrift, and they were no longer partners in crime.

Nevertheless, Leo knew he had to be clever to ensure they failed in their thievery and that all the children and Jack would escape.

Leo took a deep breath as the glow from the lantern illuminated the vast underground chamber. He closed his eyes for a moment to calm himself and then focused on his talent. He threw his voice, making it sound like it was coming from the shadows.

"Who dares disturb the resting place of Captain Jack's treasure?" His voice echoed ominously through the cave, as if it were the ghostly captain himself.

The pirates froze in terror, their eyes wide with fear, and the hurricane lamp dropped from Bart's hand, plunging the cavern into darkness. Leo continued to throw his voice, moving it around the cave, making it seem as if Captain Jack's ghost was all around them.

"I am the guardian of this treasure," Leo's voice continued, now sounding like it was right behind them. "Leave this place, or face the wrath of Captain Jack!"

Jamie was the first to run, bumping into the children

in his haste to scramble away as fast as he could. Black Bart was braver, but when he felt the breath and heard the voice of Captain Jack Swiftwater right in his ear, he too ran, scuttling after weasel face Jenkins.

Terrified and disoriented, they headed into the labyrinth of tunnels and were soon hopelessly lost. Freddie hadn't been idle while all this was happening.

"Jack!" He called his dog over and clipped on his lead.

"Are we all together?" he called. The tunnel was so devoid of light that it was impossible to see anything. Sight was useless, and only little Jack's presence ensured they would find their way out.

One by one, the children answered, and Josh sprang into action.

"Just like in the Smugglers' Tunnel," [1] he said. "Everyone take hold of the person in front of you, and I'll go first, with Jack leading the way."

"You take hold of me," instructed Harper to Summer, "and Scarlett, you take hold of your twin."

She stretched out her hand in the dark and grabbed hold of the shirt of the boy in front. "Is that you, Leo?" she asked.

"It's me," he replied, and the crocodile line of seven children made their way out, with Jack guiding them unerringly with his amazing eyesight and sense of smell through the pitch-blackness of the cave.

"What was that?" said Summer as they exited. "For a moment, I actually thought that Jack Swiftwater's ghost *was* roaming the caves!"

[1] The Adventure at Smugglers' Cove

She turned to Noz. "If you hadn't warned us…"

"Leo is the one," replied Noz. "The two of us had decided that something needed to be done once we were inside, but I had no idea what he would do!"

"He's a ventriloquist," explained Freddie, "and he can throw his voice and mimic people. It's a handy skill to have!"

"That's ingenious," said Scarlett. "You almost had me fooled. It was quite frightening hearing that voice all around."

Leo laughed. "I would love to have seen Black Bart's face when I breathed in his ear!"

"I can't see our real pirates getting out of the cave anytime soon," said Josh. "They'll be running around in the dark like headless chickens, I would think!"

"But Jamie Jenkins has the deed to the island," said Summer sadly. "Does that mean he can claim it?"

"Not at all," said Noz with a grin. "Here."

He handed a folded parchment to Summer, who opened it and stared in disbelief.

"It's the deed to the island," she said. "How?"

It was Freddie's turn to laugh. "That's a trick our Noz has up his sleeve. He's our tame criminal. A pickpocket!"

Seeing the look of dismay on their faces, Freddie quickly explained to the Cooper twins that Noz wasn't really a thief, but used his skill as a member of the Secret Six.

"When Jenkins was running around blindly in the tunnel, almost knocking us all over in his panic, I took the opportunity to relieve him of it," said Noz. Embarrassed, he took off his glasses and began to polish them intensely.

"And thanks to Jack for guiding us out," said Summer. "What a great dog. He seems to have lots of tricks, too!"

"You haven't seen the half," said Freddie proudly. "Maybe you will one day."

"We should head for home," suggested Harper, "and put these documents somewhere safe until we can get them to the authorities."

"What about the pirates?" said Scarlett.

"They can't go anywhere," said Josh. "From the sound of the collision, their boat is a write-off, and I can't see them swimming across the *Mere* back to Cooperstown, can you?"

"By the way," said Noz, "is there any food left? I'm hungry!"

And they all laughed.

Chapter Twenty-Nine

Rescue

The children assembled on the beach, surveying the wreck of the powerboat, the cabin of which was just visible just under the water.

"We can't get past that," said Summer. "I'm afraid the channel is now permanently blocked!"

"How do we get off the island, then?" asked Leo. "We're marooned like Robinson Crusoe!"

An anguished cry from Scarlett made them turn sharply to see what was wrong.

"It's our boats," she sobbed miserably. "Look what those horrid, wicked men have done to them!"

Black Bart and Jenkins had used lumps of rock to smash holes in both boats, and chunks of fragmented stone were scattered in the bottom. *Swiftwater* and *Windchaser* were lying broken on the beach, the planks of their wooden hulls destroyed.

"No!" cried Summer, "my beloved boat. How could anyone be so cruel?"

She stood hugging her twin, heartbroken at the scene before them. The boat in which they had spent so much of their childhood learning to sail, and later navigating up and down the long stretches of the *Mere,* was now only a **hulk**.

Harper stood beside them, trying to console them while struggling with her own sorrow and anger. Although it did not belong to the Secret Six, she had grown to love *Swiftwater*. The feel of the wind on her face and the sound of the gulls wheeling above as they sailed had excited her thirst for adventure like nothing else.

So there the children stood, sad, their young hearts hurting, holding each other as they sought comfort in their friendship.

Leo reached into *Swiftwater* and gathered up their flag, now muddied and torn, holding it to his chest like a prized possession.

"Tell us that poem again, Harper," he said, "The one about the lonely sea and sky."

Harper was surprised. "Only if you really want to hear it," she said reluctantly.

I must go down to the seas again, to the lonely sea and the sky,
And all I ask is a tall ship and a star to steer her by...

"Do you mind if I stop?" said Harper softly. "I can't say any more. It's too sad."

"We *will* be back on the water one day," said Freddie determinedly, "and the pirates won't stop that. You'll see," he said.

"Yes, we will," responded Summer. "Don't forget, *Swiftwater* and *Windchaser,* forever!"

✷✷✷

The beam of light cut through the darkness, and a strong voice sounded over a loudhailer.

"Ahoy, ashore," it called, "is everyone safe and well?"

Scarlett strained her eyes to see past the blinding light. "It's the coastguard cutter and police launch," she said.

"However did they know we needed help?" said Noz, surprised.

"I don't know, but we have to stop them from entering the bay," said Freddie, "or they'll be wrecked too."

"I'll warn them," said Josh. "I can easily swim out."

"That's far too dangerous," stated Freddie. "I can't let you do that."

"Scarlett or I can send a message," said Summer.

"How so?" asked Noz.

"That's one of our skills," responded Scarlett, happy to be doing something to help and take her mind off the wreckage behind her. "We can do Morse code."

"Do you have your torch?" said Summer. "The battery on mine is low."

Freddie ran to the edge of the cove and recovered it from the few items still left there, and Summer pointed it towards the boats out on the water.

"In case you don't know," said Scarlett, "we use short and long signals, like turning a light on and off, to represent letters of the alphabet and numbers."

"You turn the torch on for a short time for some letters," explained Summer, "then turn it off and back on again for a longer time for other letters."

"It's like a secret code," said Scarlett. "Summer and I use it sometimes to send messages to each other. If you write it down, you use dots for the short periods and dashes for the longer ones."

"I never thought of that," said Freddie. "Perhaps that's something the Secret Six should learn? You never know when it might come in handy."

Summer pointed the torch towards the coastguard and police boat, turning it on and off for short periods and longer ones to represent the letters of her message.

Danger. Hidden wreckage blocking channel. Do not enter. Windchaser.

She waited, and after a brief pause, a series of flashes was returned.

Windchaser. Received. Is Swiftwater with you? Coastguard.

"They want to know if you are with us," said Summer.

Yes. All OK. Windchaser.

Standby one. We are working on a plan. Coastguard over and out.

"They are working on something," said Summer. "That's going to put the cat amongst the pigeons," said Scarlett, "when our parents find out we're marooned on an island and not tucked up in bed!"

"We may as well get the rest of our tents and equipment while we wait," said Freddie, and the boys made their way up the now familiar cliff path to their camp, leaving Summer, Scarlett and Harper on the beach in case of further messages.

Jack, too, remained with the girls, and they were glad of his company. He always cheered them up when things got difficult.

It didn't take long for the others to gather everything together, and soon, they were back on the beach, where they sat to await rescue.

"I'm hungry," complained Noz, and despite their sadness, they had to smile.

Trust Noz to think of his stomach, even at a time such as this!

They found some leftover food, and there were bottles of water, which they drank gratefully. But other than Noz and Jack, no one had any appetite for eating.

Soon, the coastguard and police had worked out a plan, and using a flat-bottomed rubber dinghy, they ferried the children and their dog in small groups to the waiting rescue craft, where they were wrapped in blankets as they had begun to shiver.

"It's the shock," said the coastguard boatman, "but you'll be okay."

"How did you know we needed help?" said Freddie.

"The emergency fire on top of the castle," he replied.

"That was good thinking, youngsters," said the police officer. "The blaze could be seen for miles."

Harper said nothing but inwardly felt uncomfortable.

"What about the pirates?" said Summer.

"Pirates?" asked the startled police officer.

She explained about the map and Captain Jack Swiftwater's treasure and how Black Bart and Jamie Jenkins had plotted to steal it.

"Is that Jamie 'The Weasel' Jenkins?" said the police officer.

"It is. Oh, and please be careful. Black Bart has got a gun," she said.

"We don't know a Black Bart," said the police officer after conferring with the coastguard. "He must be from out of town. Anyway, don't you worry about them, they won't be going anywhere. We'll collect them in the morning when it's daylight."

"They aren't that bright then," said the coastguard with a reassuring smile.

"And the treasure?" said Summer.

"That sounds far-fetched," said the police officer doubtfully, "but I know you, Miss Summer, and although you can be wild, I have never found you to be a liar, so we'll take care of your treasure too until it can all be sorted out."

"You'll need one of us to show you the cave," explained Freddie. "It's well-hidden."

"Tomorrow will be soon enough," said the officer. "We'll put an officer on the island in the meantime to ensure everything is safe and secure."

He signalled to the coastguard cutter, and they headed away from Shadowmere Island towards Cooperstown and home, and soon the seven children and Jack were fast asleep below deck.

```
A • —        N — •
B — • • •    O — — —
C — • — •    P • — — •
D — • •      Q — — • —
E •          R • — •
F • • — •    S • • •
G — — •      T —
H • • • •    U • • —
I • •        V • • • —
J • — — —    W • — —
K — • —      X — • • —
L • — • •    Y — • — —
M — —        Z — — • •
```

MORSE CODE

Chapter Thirty

Coming Together

"Why don't you go outside?" Mrs. Lyon suggested, noticing how Harper and Leo seemed **apathetic**. They were sitting inside their house on a weekend, feeling bored. They had been back at school for a few weeks after their exciting adventure in Cumbria. Their friends, the Dubois twins, had settled in at Swiftwater Cottage and attended a new school. They really missed them, along with dear little Jack and also the new friends they had made, Summer and Scarlett.

"I think it's an idea to go out," their mum insisted. "I don't want you littering the place up or getting under my feet."

Reluctantly, Harper and Leo got up and headed towards the front door. Without their friends, everything just seemed kind of gloomy. They had met up with Noz a few times, but he was feeling down too, so their group, the Secret Six, had turned into just three tired friends—the Lethargic Three.

When they opened the door, it surprised them to see Noz standing there.

"Hi, Noz," Leo greeted him. "What's going on? Is everything okay?"

Noz had a strange expression, and it seemed like he had some exciting news.

"It's fantastic!" Noz exclaimed.

Out of nowhere, a bolt of black energy shot down the driveway and threw himself at Harper and Leo, making little cries of happiness and wagging his tail furiously.

"Jack!" shouted Harper, dropping to her knees and burying her face in his soft fur. "Oh, I've missed you so much!"

"*Et nous*—what about us?" said Josh and Freddie simultaneously.

"And us!" exclaimed Summer and Scarlett.

Harper and Leo were so surprised and thrilled to see their dear friends again that they couldn't believe their eyes for a moment. And, immediately, all their sadness turned to pure happiness.

Harper felt overwhelming joy seeing Summer wearing another red woollen hat, just as she remembered, positioned confidently on her head like a buccaneer.

"I see you're still wearing my hat," observed Summer, "and you've got it about right now!" Still, she couldn't resist making a tiny adjustment to it. "There," she said, "now it's perfect!"

Harper couldn't speak. She embraced the dearest and best of friends she had ever known and was content to hold on to them as the tears coursed down all their faces.

"You can all come in if you would like to," said Mrs Lyon, wiping her eyes with her apron. "I've got some food ready, Noz," she laughed.

Sitting in the living room, some on chairs and the others spilling over onto the floor, the children could hardly believe they were together again.

"Do tell," said Harper, absolutely bursting with

excitement. "The pirates, *Swiftwater, Windchaser,* the treasure, the island—everything!"

Freddie glanced at Summer and Scarlett. "I think you should be the ones to update them," he said. "After all, it's your story."

"Tell us about the treasure," said Leo. "I've been so longing to hear about it."

Summer laughed. "Let's start at the beginning. Or perhaps it's the end," she said, and took a deep breath.

"The important thing was the island," she said. "In his will, Captain Jack Swiftwater made it clear that whoever owned the island owned everything. The house and the treasure. It took forever for the court to look at the documents and decide. Finally, they said that Jack Swiftwater's wishes were clear enough. He wanted whoever found his will to become heir to Shadowmere."

"And don't forget," said Scarlett, "the letter he wrote confessing to stealing William Cooper's money. That was a big plus in the court's decision!"

"So, you own an island?" said Noz in excitement.

"Well," responded Scarlett. "After talking it through with our family, they all agreed that we don't have a right to just take it after all that has happened."

"That's a shame," said Harper. "But I think I understand." She sounded disappointed.

Summer's face lit up. "I don't think you do. We've given nearly all of it to the most courageous and kindest friends in the world!"

She handed Harper and Leo an official-looking paper.

"Look at the names on the top," encouraged Scarlett excitedly.

Harper took it, her hands trembling as she read. "It says; Summer Cooper, Scarlett Cooper, Freddie Dubois, Joshua Dubois, Noah Khumalo, Harper Lyon, Leo Lyon, and Jack the Dog!"

"Is that for real?" spluttered Leo. "Are we really part owners of an island?"

"We are," responded Summer. "We each own one-eighth, and you deserve it more than anyone I can think of. Without you all, the will and the treasure would never have been found."

"Can a dog own part of an island?" asked Noz. "I seem to remember…"

"We know!" responded Summer and Scarlett gleefully. "You learned something about it in school!"

Noz removed his glasses and polished them energetically. "I didn't. Not this time. I read it somewhere," he laughed.

"We don't know the legal side," continued Scarlett. "But we told the solicitor we wanted Jack on the deed, so she put him on. Summer insisted, and she can be quite fierce!"

Harper smiled. "I don't know how we can ever thank you. All of us—The Secret Six. We never expected anything and just wanted to help you restore old William Cooper's good name."

"That brings us onto the next part of the tale," said Scarlett.

She turned to Freddie and Josh. "You're unusually quiet. Do you want to say anything?"

"*Absolument rien*—nothing," said Josh. "It's your

214

story—yours and Summer's, and I'm enjoying hearing it all again."

"Same goes for me," agreed Freddie. "I'm liking Harper and Leo's look of astonishment."

"I'm sure you want to hear about the treasure," said Scarlett. "Summer, you're better than I am at explaining things."

"A special court had to sit and decide whether it was ours," responded Summer.

"It was the Coroner for Treasure," explained Scarlett.

"It was all complicated law," continued Summer, "but our solicitor was outstanding and explained everything to the court brilliantly."

"And?" said Leo.

"And it's ours! Or at least the Cooper family's," responded Summer.

"Gosh, you must be very rich," said Leo.

"The family has given most of it away," said Scarlett. "Quite a lot went to a London museum, and we've given some to our local council to renovate some of the poorer areas."

"Mum and Dad are forming a charitable trust," said Summer, "in William Cooper's name, to help the less fortunate."

"I'm not surprised," said Harper. "That's just the thing you would do. We're so proud of you."

"What about the pirates? What happened to them?" asked Leo impatiently.

"That's an interesting story," said Scarlett. "The police had to send some caving specialists to find them. There were so many labyrinths that Black Bart and Jamie Jenkins had gotten totally lost in the dark.

By the time they were found, they were so terrified that they almost threw themselves into the arms of the police!"

Summer laughed. "The poor arresting officers didn't know what to say. Those hardened criminals were going on and on about Captain Swiftwater's ghost!"

"So all's well that ends well," said Scarlett. "What do you think, Noz? And Harper and Leo?"

"We're so pleased for you," said Harper. "To have the family reputation restored is a fantastic thing."

"You don't sound all that happy," observed Summer. "Could it be because you miss Freddie, Josh, and little Jack?"

"Oh, I do!" said Harper. "And you and Scarlett. More than I can say. But I am trying to come to terms with it. And I'm glad that they have you as friends up there in the wilds of Cumbria."

"That's the next bit of excitement," said Freddie, who hadn't spoken for some time and had been struggling to contain his eagerness. "We're moving back here!"

"Back here?" responded Harper, her eyes wide. "Really? You and Josh and Jack? The Secret Six reunited?"

Freddie nodded.

"*C'est vrai*—It's true," said Josh.

"But how?" asked Leo. "You said your dad couldn't afford the price of houses here."

Freddie and Josh looked across to Summer and Scarlett, who were doing their best to become invisible.

"We have some wonderful friends," he said. "What more can I say?"

They sat in silence for a while, digesting the volume

216

of exciting news.

"One last thing," said Harper. "*Swiftwater* and *Windchaser*?"

"Repaired!" said Summer. "Good as new. Our local boatbuilder mended both, and *Swiftwater* is waiting for you when you come to see us on your next holiday."

Freddie unfolded a piece of cloth from his pocket and held it up.

"Look," he said, "mended by my mum and as good as new. Ready for our next adventure!"

It was *Swiftwater's* flag.

And that's how it all came together. Those were the days of incredible friendships, endless laughter, and thrilling adventures they'd cherish forever. Years from now, they would fondly remember those times and feel grateful for the wild and daring things they did as children. They had bravely stared danger and challenges in the face, even when their hearts had raced with fear. But they hadn't just survived; they had thrived.

Because when it truly counted, they had stood by each other's side, unwavering and strong.

Swiftwater and *Windchaser*: forever and ever!

Glossary

WORD	MEANING
Acrid	Unpleasant, Choking
Antics	Playfulness
Apathetic	Droopy, Lazy
Befuddled	Confused
Blockade	Barrier, Block
Brig	Prison on a boat
Browsing	Looking
Bureau	Chest of drawers
Camaraderie	Friendship
Castellated	Battlements
Catastrophe	Disaster
Charade	Fake
Circumnavigate	Sail around
Clarity	Clearness
Claustrophobic	Oppressive, Shut-in
Cleat	To tie a boat to
Companionway	A set of steps and hatch from the cabin of a boat
Complied	Obeyed
Condescendingly	Sneeringly
Contemplated	Thought
Contrite	Sorry
Coveted	Desirable
Cowed	Scared
Decipher	Translate
Digit	Finger
Disconsolate	Sad, Dejected
Downhaul Line	For pulling down a sail

Edifice	A structure
Elongated	Stretched
Emphasising	Highlighting
En-route	French word – on the way
Escalate	Increase
Fore	Front (of a boat)
Formidable	Awesome
Founder	Sink, Submerge
Gorge	Ravine, Valley
Gunwale	Where the sides of a boat meet the deck
Gybe	When the boom of a boat sweeps across
Halyard	Rope
Helm	Tiller, Steering wheel
Hoarded	Hid, Stashed away
Huffed	Grumbled
Hulk	Wreck, Remains
Impediment	Obstruction, Barrier
Imperative	Urgent, Crucial
Imperceptibly	Unnoticeably, Invisibly
Impoverished	Poor, Hard-up
Incredulous	Doubtful, Suspicious
Insatiable	Limitless, Greedy
intoxicating	Exhilarating, Heady
Irately	Angrily, Crossly
Jib	Small front sail of boat
Labyrinthine	Complex, Intricate
Lanyards	Cords
Lee	Shelter, Cover
Listed	Tilted, Sloped, Leaned

Maliciously	Wickedly, spitefully
Marooned	Stranded, Isolated, Left
Mimic	Copycat
Momentum	Force, Motion, Energy
Ominously	Worryingly, Gloomily
Painter	Front rope on a boat to tie it to a mooring
Parallel	Side by side, In the same direction, Match
Pea Coat	Worn by sailors in olden times
Perilous	Dangerous, Risky
Port	Left side of a boat
Presided	Supervised, Chaired
Proffered	Offered, Gave
Pulmonary	Lung, Respiratory
Quay	Dock, Harbour, Pier
Ransom	Exchange, Release,
Recluse	Solitary, Hermit
Reef	Gather a portion of sail to reduce its size
Rotund	Stout, Plump
Rowlocks	Oarlocks to hold the oars when rowing
Run before the wind	Sailing with the wind directly behind the boat
RV	Rendezvous – meet up
Sabotaged	Damage, Disrupt
Sauntered	Strolled, Wandered
Schooner	Large sailing ship
Scull	Paddle, Row

Shrouds	Lines holding up a mast or sail
Silted	Fill with sand or mud
Sophistication	Refined, Elegant, Chic
Stanchions	Legs, Pillars, Columns
Starboard	The right side of a boat
Stepped	Set the mast of a boat in place ready for the sails
Stowed	Store away
Tack	Zigzag to catch the wind in a sail
Tentatively	Cautiously, Hesitantly
Thwart	Seats on a small boat
Traverse	Navigate, Negotiate, Go across
Trepidation	Fear, anxiety, unease
Twenty-thirty hours	8.30 pm 24-hour clock
Ventriloquist	Usually an entertainer with a talking puppet
Verge	Grass at side of road
Villain	Criminal, Baddy,
Volume	Book, Tome, Edition
Voracious	Greedy, Big, Glutton
Wry	Cynical, Dry humour

Last things…

Please consider leaving a review on Amazon about my book.

Thank You!

Stephen Nuttall

Printed in Great Britain
by Amazon

36131711R00126